the reluctant *princess*

Her Royal Duty, Book Two

MELISSA McCLONE

Cardinal Press, LLC
April 2019
ISBN-13: 9781944777289

Dedication

For Tom, Mackenna, Finn, Rose,
Chaos, Maat, Yoda, Beauty, and Cato.
The best family a writer could have!

Special thanks to:
Elizabeth Boyle, Drew Brayshaw, Roger Carstens,
Adaline Fraser, John Fenzel, Terri Reed,
Robert Wilhams, and Camas Physical Therapy.

Chapter One

Crown Prince Nikola Tomislav Kresimir of Vernonia strode past his father's assistant and the two palace guards standing watch. As soon as he entered the king's office, the door closed behind him.

He grimaced.

Niko didn't have time for another impromptu assignment. Thousands of unread emails filled his inbox. The upcoming trade conference was becoming a logistical nightmare. Princess Julianna of Aliestle sat patiently in the library, waiting to have lunch with him.

His title demanded he juggle competing

responsibilities. He thrived on doing that, but the collar of his dress shirt seemed to have shrunk two inches since he'd left his office three minutes ago. He tugged on his tie.

Not that doing anything would lessen his frustration level.

A summons from the king trumped everything else and often messed up Niko's schedule for the rest of the day, sometimes the week. Not to mention, the havoc royal protocol played with his priority of turning their provincial country into a modern nation. But he followed his father's orders out of respect and for the good of Vernonia.

King Dmitar sat behind his massive mahogany desk staring at a manila file folder in his hands. His once dark hair was now as white as the snowcapped peaks of the Balkans and Carpathians. His face, like Niko's, was as rugged as those same mountain ranges. His wire-rimmed reading glasses rested low on his nose, making him seem more like a professor than a soldier and a king who had spent most of his rule trying to unite his country against all odds.

Niko stood ten feet away, waiting.

A breeze blew through an open window, carrying the sweet fragrance of flowers from the royal gardens. A vast improvement over the acrid smell of gunpowder and the sickening scent of blood that used to taint the air.

Five years had passed since the ratification of the

peace treaty. Tensions between the two warring factions erupted occasionally, but peace prevailed. Niko intended to ensure it always would. That was what his late older brother, Stefan, would have wanted. A united Vernonia, however, seemed like a far-off dream. A fairy tale, really.

Not wanting to waste more time, Niko cleared his throat.

His father glanced up. Dark circles ringed his eyes.

"You sent for me, sir," Niko said in English, which many citizens spoke. He and his father were trying to get out of the habit of speaking their native Slavic language because of the princess staying at the castle. If things worked out as he hoped, she would soon be living here permanently.

The lines on his father's face seemed deeper, more pronounced, than they used to be. The conflict had aged him. So had grief. But the corners of his mouth curved upward into a rare smile. "I have good news, my son."

The best news would be a line of credit assured by European banks. Improvement projects needed to be completed to move the country forward.

Niko stepped closer to the oversized desk. "I've spent the morning wading through the demands of the trade delegations. Good news will be a welcome relief, Father."

"I have located your bride box."

The unexpected news sank in. Resonated through

him.

Niko respected the past—honored history as best he could—but the fact his marriage depended on the antiquated custom of presenting his wife a family heirloom on their wedding day irritated him. Traditions could only take his country so far. The new millennium required change. That included mindsets. But if he had the box, he could take the required steps to assure Vernonia's future.

A thrill shot through him.

Even though his father knew how much locating the family treasure meant to Niko, he struggled not to show any emotion. Emotion was a weakness. His father had been telling him that his entire life. "You are certain the box is mine?"

"As certain as we can be until we see it in person."

That was closer than they'd been before.

Niko released the breath he'd been holding. His bride box had disappeared over twenty years ago when terrorist acts led to a deadly civil war that ripped the country apart and nearly destroyed it. The economy had yet to recover.

"Where is the box?" he asked.

"The United States." His father adjusted his glasses and studied the folder. "Charlotte, North Carolina."

"A long way from home."

"Yes."

The location wasn't important. What mattered was Niko would have possession of the box soon.

Tradition—and his father—would be satisfied. Nothing would stand in the way of Niko's marriage to Julianna. He could finally fulfill his duty as his parents and people wished him to do. The marriage would give him the means, courtesy of the princess's dowry, and opportunity, provided by her country's alliances, to do what he wanted—needed—to do with Vernonia.

Plans formed in his mind, but he couldn't get too far ahead of himself. First, he needed the box. "How was it discovered?"

"The internet." His father shuffled through papers in the file. "Someone posted on an antiques forum, searching for the key. After exchanges verifying the seriousness of our interest, the person emailed a photo that confirmed our suspicions. The box is yours."

"Incredible." Niko considered the numerous private investigators and treasure hunters hired to find the missing heirloom. He laughed at the irony. "Technology to the rescue of an Old World custom."

"Technology may be useful, but our people desire tradition. You must remember that when you wear the crown."

"Everything I've done has been for Vernonia." Niko's family had ruled for eight centuries. The country was in their blood and hearts. Duty always came first. "I realize the importance of the bride box to our country, but we must modernize if we are to succeed in the twenty-first century."

His father studied Niko. "Yet you have agreed to

an arranged marriage."

"I have always known my bride would be decided for me. That is our way."

But in this case, he was pleased with the choice. His marriage to Julianna wasn't a love match, but he respected the princess and considered her a friend. Something he couldn't say about every royal presented to him as a potential wife. Perhaps love would grow as the years passed. No matter, their marriage would act as a bridge between the past and the future.

He might not be as popular as the United Kingdom's Prince William or Prince Harry, but Niko had the attention of royal watchers. The publicity surrounding a royal wedding would be good for his country's nascent tourist industry. He would use whatever he could to Vernonia's advantage, including his marriage. "I may not be a stickler for tradition, but I will always do what is best for the country."

"As will I." His father placed the folder on his desk. "You have the key."

"Of course, sir." Niko had been wearing the idiotic thing for twenty-odd years, ever since the decree that never allowed him to take it off. Only the size of the chain had changed.

He pulled the thick silver necklace from beneath his shirt. The key resembling a cross and heart welded together dangled from his fingers. "Can I stop wearing it now?"

"No." The word echoed through the spacious

office until the tapestries on the wall swallowed the sound. "You will need the key when you go to North Carolina tomorrow."

"Send Jovan. I can't travel to the United States. I'm needed here," Niko countered. "My schedule is full. Princess Julianna is visiting."

"The box is yours." His father used his majestic tone, the one that demanded immediate compliance. "You will bring it home. My assistant will provide your aide with a travel itinerary and information."

Niko bit his tongue. Further resistance would be futile. Even if it made little sense under the current circumstances, the king's say was final. "Fine, but you realize I have never seen the box."

"You have seen it. You were a child, so you don't remember."

What Niko remembered was war, the one thing he wanted and hoped to forget. The cost of the conflict had been immeasurable with the loss of lives, including that of the crown prince, his brother and best friend. Not a day went by that he didn't think of Stefan.

Miss him.

Keeping peace and modernizing Vernonia were Niko's only goals. Though the parliament wanted him to provide an heir. Now that nothing stood in his way of marrying, he could soon tackle that request. Speaking of which...

"Do you wish for me to propose to Julianna before I leave for America or upon my return, Father?"

The king's face reddened. "There shall be no official proposal."

"What?" Niko remembered the open window and the people on the other side of the office door. He lowered his voice. "We've spent months negotiating with the Council of Elders in Aliestle. Even the Separatists are in favor of the marriage since King Alaric supported them during the conflict. The only obstacle has been the bride box. A delay will send the wrong—"

"No proposal."

Frustration mounted. Niko had searched for a suitable bride for over a year. He didn't want to start over. "You agreed Julianna is an excellent choice for a wife and the future queen of Vernonia. That is why finding the box has been a priority."

"Julianna is more than suitable to be the queen, but..." His father removed his glasses and rubbed his eyes. "Are you in love with her?"

Love? His traditional father broaching the subject surprised Niko. His grandparents had arranged his parents' marriage. After Stefan's death, Niko had stepped into his role as crown prince. The choice of his bride—a woman who would be queen—had become more complicated now that he would rule, but that was his fate.

"We get along well. Share common views and have a similar sense of responsibility. She's beautiful and intelligent. I will be content with her as my wife," Niko stated honestly. "The publicity surrounding a royal wedding will increase our visibility to the tourist industry. Most importantly, an alliance with Aliestle will give Vernonia the capital required to complete rebuilding. I see no negatives or problems with this union."

"You've examined all angles."

Niko bowed his head. "As you taught me, Father."

"And Julianna. Are her feelings engaged?"

"She...cares for me," Niko answered carefully. "As I do for her. She understands what is expected."

"But is she in love with you?"

Uncomfortable, Niko shifted his weight between his feet. "You've never spoken about love before. Only duty and what a state marriage would entail."

"You are old enough to know whether a woman has feelings for you or not. Answer my question."

Niko considered his outing with Julianna yesterday. They'd left their security detail on the shore and sailed on the lake. He'd kissed her for the first time. The kiss had been...pleasant, but Julianna appeared more interested in sailing than in kissing him again. "I do not believe she is in love with me. In fact, I'm certain she isn't."

"Good."

"I do not understand what is going on, sir. If something has changed with Vernonia's relationship to Aliestle—"

"Nothing has changed." His father's drawn-out

sigh would have made the parliament members' knees tremble beneath their heavy robes. "But a slight...complication in regard to you marrying Julianna has arisen."

Niko's muscles tensed. "What kind of complication?"

Chapter Two

Inside Bay Number Two at Rowdy's One Stop Garage in Charlotte, North Carolina, a Brad Paisley song blared from a nearby radio. Oil, gasoline, and grease scented the air. Isabel Poussard bent over a Chevy 350 small block engine. The bolt she needed to remove wouldn't budge, but she wasn't giving up or asking for help. She wanted the guys to see her as an equal, not a woman who couldn't make it on her own.

She adjusted the wrench. "Come on now. Turn for Izzy."

A swatch of brown hair fell across her face so she

couldn't see.

Stupid ponytail. Strands always fell out.

If she had any extra money, she would visit a hair salon and have them cut off the length. She didn't dare try it herself. For years, her uncle Frank had chopped her hair with whatever was handy, scissors or razor blades. She'd grown up looking more like a boy than a girl. Not that any dresses hung in her closet today.

Izzy tucked the stray pieces behind her ear. As she struggled with the wrench, her sweaty palm made it slip. Frustrated, she blew out a puff of air. "No one will let you work over the wall during a race if you can't loosen a little bolt."

She imagined the start of the Daytona 500. The roar of the crowd. The heat from the pavement. The smell of burning rubber. The rev of engines.

Excitement surged through her.

Being on a professional pit crew had been Uncle Frank's dream for as long as Izzy remembered. An aneurysm had cut his life short. Now, it was up to her to make his dream into a reality. He'd spent his life caring for her and sharing his skill and love of cars. More than once, he'd had the opportunity to join a race team, but he hadn't wanted to leave her. This was the least she could do for him.

As soon as Izzy saved enough money, she would enroll in a pit crew school. She wanted to put her days at dirt tracks and stock car circuits behind her and take a shot at the big leagues.

For Uncle Frank and herself.

She had bigger goals than being on a pit crew. She wanted to be the crew chief. Izzy would show those kids who laughed at her grease-stained hands they were wrong. She would do something with her life.

Something big.

She adjusted her grip on the wrench and tried again. The bolt moved. "Yes!"

"Hey, Izzy," the garage owner's son and her closest friend, Boyd, shouted to her over the Lady Antebellum song now playing. "Some folks here to see you."

Word of mouth about her skills kept spreading. She not only fixed old engines, but hybrids, too. Her understanding of the computer and electronics side of things coupled with a gift for diagnostics drew in new clients daily. Her boss, Rowdy, was so happy he'd given Izzy a raise. If this kept up, she could enroll in school come fall.

With a smile, she placed her wrench and the bolt on her toolbox.

As soon as Izzy stepped outside, fresh air filled her lungs. Sunshine warmed her face. She loved spring days better than the humid ones summer brought.

In front of her, a black limousine gleamed beneath the midday sun. The engine idled perfectly. Darkened windows hid the identity of the car's passengers, but uniformed police officers stood nearby.

Not "some folks" wanting to see her. Must be a VIP inside the limo if they needed police escorts.

Izzy couldn't imagine what they wanted with her since the car sounded like it was running fine.

She wiped her dirty hands on the thighs of her cotton coveralls. Not exactly clean, especially with grease caked under her fingernails, but cleaner.

An officer gave her the once-over as if sizing up her danger potential. A good thing she'd left the wrench in the garage.

A chauffeur came around the car and opened the rear door. A blond man exited. He wore a designer suit and polished black dress shoes. With a classically handsome face and short clipped hair, he was easy on the eyes. But his good looks seemed a little bland, like a bowl of vanilla ice cream with no hot fudge, whipped cream, and candy sprinkles. She preferred men who weren't so pretty, men with a little more...character.

"Isabel Poussard?" the man asked.

She stiffened. The last time anyone used her real name had been during her high school graduation ceremony when she'd received her diploma. She'd always been Izzy, ever since she was a little girl. Uncle Frank had taught her to be careful and cautious around strangers. He'd worried about her and been protective. She knew he'd be that way now if he were here.

Izzy raised her chin and stared down her nose. The gesture had sent more than one guy running in the opposite direction. "Who wants to know?"

Warm brown eyes met hers. The guy wasn't intimidated. If anything, he appeared amused. "I am

Jovan Novak, aide to His Royal Highness Crown Prince Nikola Tomislav Kresimir."

Jovan's accent sounded European. Interesting since this was NASCAR country, not Formula 1 territory. "Never heard of him."

"He's from Vernonia."

"Vernonia." The name sounded vaguely familiar. Suddenly, Izzy remembered. "That's one of those Balkan countries. Fairy-tale castles and snowcapped mountains. There was a civil war there."

"Yes."

"Hey, Izzy," Boyd shouted from behind her. "You need any help?"

The bear of a man stood with a mallet in one hand and curiosity on his face. She appreciated how Boyd treated her like a little sister, especially since she had no family. That had made things interesting the few times a date picked her up after work. "Not yet, Boyd, but I'll let you know if I do."

Jovan appeared to be in shape, but she could take him without Boyd's help, thanks to Uncle Frank. When she was younger, he'd bartered his mechanic skills for her martial arts class tuition. Now she worked out every day to get in shape for the work required by a pit crew member during a race.

"Isabel. Izzy." Smiling, Jovan bowed. "It is such a pleasure to make your acquaintance, Your—"

"Is this about a car repair?" He acted so happy to meet her. That bothered Izzy. Most customers limited their interactions to questions about their cars. Some ignored her. A few men propositioned her. "Or do you want something else? I'm in the middle of a job."

Not exactly the most friendly customer service, but something felt *off*. No customer would know her real name. And the guy smiled too much to be having car trouble.

"One moment, please." With a smile still on his face, Jovan ducked into the limousine.

Time ticked by. Seconds or minutes, Izzy couldn't tell since she wasn't wearing a watch. She used her cell phone to keep track of time while she worked. But that was on her toolbox.

Izzy tapped her foot. She had to finish the Chevy so she could work on the Dodge Grand Caravan. Somewhere a frazzled mom with four kids was waiting for her minivan to be repaired. It was up to Izzy to get the job done.

Jovan stepped out of the limo finally.

About time.

Another man in a dark suit followed.

Smokin'.

The thought shot from Izzy's brain to the tips of her steel-toed boots and ricocheted to the top of her head.

The guy was at least six feet tall with thick, shoulder-length brown hair and piercing blue-green eyes framed by dark lashes.

She straightened as if an extra inch could bring her

closer to his height. Her head barely came to his chin.

But what a chin.

Izzy swallowed a sigh.

A strong nose, chiseled cheekbones, dark brows. The rugged features made for an interesting—handsome—combination despite a jagged scar on his right cheek.

Talk about character. He had it in spades.

Not that she was interested.

Spending her entire life surrounded by men—car mechanics—gave her an understanding of how the opposite sex thought and operated. The one standing in front of her wearing a tailored suit and shiny shoes was trouble.

Dangerous, too.

The limo, expensive clothing, personal aide, and police escort meant he lived in a different world than her, a world where she was viewed as nothing more than a servant or wallpaper or worse, a one-night stand. Having to deal with mysterious rich people intimidated her. She wanted nothing to do with him.

Though she didn't mind taking another look. The man belonged on the cover of a glossy men's magazine. He moved with the grace and agility of an athlete. The fit of his suit made her wonder what muscles he had underneath the fancy fabric.

She couldn't remember the last time she'd reacted this way to a man. No doubt the result of working too much overtime. Time to take a night off and have fun.

That would keep her from mooning over the next gorgeous guy who crossed her path.

"You are Isabel Poussard." His accent, a mix of British and something else, could melt a frozen stick of butter.

She nodded, not trusting her voice.

His assessing gaze traveled the length of her. Nothing in his expression hinted at what he might think about her.

Not that she cared. Not much anyway.

A hottie would never be interested in a grease monkey. Still, he was a yummy piece of eye candy. One she could appreciate.

Izzy raised her chin again, but she didn't stare down her nose the way she'd done with Jovan. She wasn't ready to send this one on his way yet. "You know my name, but I don't know yours."

"I am Prince Nikola of Vernonia."

"A prince?"

"Yes."

She supposed a prince would have a police escort and an aide, but this was the kind of joke Boyd would pull and kid Izzy about for the rest of her life. She searched for a camera. "Am I being pranked?"

Jovan grinned.

Nikola pressed his lips together. "No."

Yeah, on second thought, she couldn't imagine the police participating in a joke. But she had a hard time believing royalty would be at Rowdy's. This wasn't the sketchiest part of town, but it wasn't the best, either. "Am I supposed to call you Your Highness or something?"

"Niko is fine."

Better than fine, but he probably knew that. Men as attractive as him usually did. "So, Niko, why are you here?"

Jovan started to speak, but Niko held up his hand and silenced his aide.

Nice trick. Maybe he was a prince. Or maybe he enjoyed being the one to talk.

"You posted on the internet searching for a key," Niko said. "The box is mine."

"I don't think so, dude."

He winced.

"It belonged to my mother," Izzy added. "I just want the key."

"I know, but the box in the picture never belonged to your mother."

Oh, boy. Rowdy and Boyd had told Izzy if she posted on the internet she would receive strange responses. But she'd received only one reply from a person who described the box so perfectly she'd sent him a picture of it. "You're H-R-M-K-D-K?"

"That's my father," Niko explained. "His Royal Majesty King Dmitar Kresimir."

Like a king would email a total stranger about a wooden box. Sure, it was pretty, but it was old. Izzy thought the only value was sentimental. Maybe she was wrong about its worth. "I corresponded with your, um, dad, but I told you, the box belongs to me."

"The box is technically yours, but only because I gave it to you."

What a ridiculous statement. The box was her only link to her mother who had died when Izzy was a baby. That was why she was desperate to find the missing key and open the bottom portion to see if anything was inside. With Uncle Frank gone, she had no family, no connection to her past. She wanted to know something...anything.

Fighting her disappointment over not finding the key, Izzy squared her shoulders. "I've heard of Vernonia, but I've never been there. I'm certain we've never met. I've had the box for as long as I can remember."

"You have had the box for twenty-three years. I gave it to you when you were a baby."

"A baby," she repeated as if hearing it again would make more sense than the first time. It didn't. The guy wasn't that much older than her—that would mean he'd been a kid, too. Ridiculous.

"Yes," Niko admitted ruefully. "I must sound crazy."

If he wasn't, then she was. "You do."

"I can assure you I'm not crazy," Niko stated matter-of-factly. "Isn't that true, Jovan?"

"Not crazy," Jovan agreed, though he continued to seem amused by the situation.

"I'm guessing you're paid to agree with him, Jovan," Izzy said, irritated.

"Yes, but I'm also a lawyer if that adds to my credibility."

"It doesn't." Maybe this was how attractive, eccentric royals wasted their time and money. She wished they would go bother someone else. "I think you both must be certifiable."

The two men stared at her with puzzled expressions.

"Insane." Izzy couldn't imagine police officers wasting tax dollars protecting a mental case claiming to be a prince. Surely they would have checked him out and asked to see his diplomatic papers or passport. "Let's pretend what you say is true—"

"It is true," Niko said.

She took a deep breath to control her growing temper. "Why would you give a baby the box? Is there some significance to the gesture?"

"It's customary."

This made no sense. "Huh?"

"Tradition," Niko clarified. "When a Vernonian prince gets married, he presents his wife with a bride box on their wedding day."

"That still doesn't explain why you would give me the box."

"Because I am your husband."

Chapter Three

"My husband?" Isabel's voice cracked. Her expression would have been comical if this wasn't such a serious matter.

"Yes." Niko understood her shock. He sympathized with her. Discovering he had a wife had sent his world spinning off its axis. But Isabel's feelings—his feelings—would only delay the annulment needed to remedy this "complication" so he could marry Julianna and help his country. "It is a lot to take in."

"Take in?" A sharp gaze bore into him. "Okay,

Niko or whoever you are, cut the bull and tell me what's really going on here."

He stared at Isabel with the dirty, baggy coveralls, lopsided ponytail, and grease on her hands and cheek. She might be halfway attractive with her oval face, high cheekbones, and expressive eyes, if she wasn't dressed like a man and covered in motor oil.

"Come on, Niko." She raised her chin. "Spill."

He expected her lack of protocol and manners, but the strength in her voice surprised him, as did her take-no-prisoners tone. Most people kowtowed to him. Few challenged him. He was...intrigued. "I am speaking the truth. I am your husband."

She pursed her full, unglossed lips and gave him a long, hard stare.

He was used to frank appraisals, but unlike most women, Isabel did not seem impressed by him. He didn't know whether to be amused or annoyed by this woman who worked at a dilapidated garage, fixing other people's broken-down vehicles.

"I told you. I've never seen you before," she said. "We can't be married."

"Indeed, we can. You do not remember."

Isabel's expression of disbelief remained steady. "I'd remember getting married."

"Not if you were only a few months old."

Her mouth formed a perfect O. "What?"

"I was six years old when we wed, and my memories are vague."

Almost nonexistent, but he needed to convince Isabel of what had happened, not add to the doubts shining in her hazel eyes.

"Children marrying?" Isabel's nostrils flared. "There are laws against that kind of thing."

"Yes, but it was an archaic custom only to be used in extreme circumstances. Today, it's illegal in Vernonia, but not twenty-three years ago."

"This is crazy." Her voice jumped an octave. "I'm an American."

"Your mother was American, but your father was Vernonian."

"My father..." Isabel angled her shoulders toward Jovan as if seeking confirmation. At his nod, her hands balled into fists. "Now I know you're lying. My father's name isn't listed on my birth certificate. I have no idea who he is."

The hurt and anger in her voice suggested she was telling the truth. She had no reason to lie. Not when she had so much to gain by accepting what Niko was telling her. His respect inched up. Opportunists or not, many women would have jumped at the chance to be his wife. "I have proof."

"You mean the box."

"The bride box, yes, but also documentation."

Curiosity flashed on Isabel's face. "What kind of documentation?"

Her interest loosened some tension in his shoulders. Maybe the paper would convince her of the truth. He motioned to Jovan, who removed a leather pouch from his inside suit pocket with a flourish and handed it over.

As Niko opened the flap, he noticed two tall men in coveralls watching them from the garage.

No doubt the limousine and police cars would attract a second glance. Niko wanted to avoid the media at all cost. The annulment needed to be handled quietly with no press coverage.

Before departing for the United States, he had told Julianna about the situation, but others might not be as understanding about the sudden appearance of "his wife" on the front page of tabloids. He didn't want to risk losing the beautiful and wealthy princess from Aliestle given what she would bring to Vernonia.

He scanned the parking lot and garage. They were drawing people's attention. "I would prefer a more private place to discuss matters. Inside the limo perhaps?"

Isabel glared at him. "Do I look like a woman who would get into a car with strangers?"

Niko assumed based on her reaction the answer wasn't yes. "I may be a stranger, but I am your husband."

"That remains to be seen."

She wasn't making this easy, but given her appearance he shouldn't be surprised. "Perhaps there is an office in the garage we could use."

"Here."

He needed her cooperation. The last thing Niko wanted to do was upset her more than he had. He would allow her this much control.

"Fine. We shall remain here." He removed two folded pieces of paper from the pouch. "I had our marriage certificate translated."

She eyed him warily. "Marriage certificate, huh?"

He extended the papers toward her. "See for yourself."

Instead of reaching for the documents as Niko expected, Isabel wiped her hands on the thighs of her oversized coveralls. The same way she had when she walked out of the garage.

Not totally without manners, but a far cry from the grace and style of Julianna, who had been raised to be a queen. "These are copies so it doesn't matter if they get dirty."

Isabel took the documents and unfolded them. As she read, she flipped between the two pages.

Niko appreciated her thoroughness. Now he needed her compliance. Given how things were proceeding so far, that might take time. Especially since he hadn't explained the entire situation to her.

"The certificate looks legit," she said.

"It is."

"But it's wrong." She pointed her oil-stained finger to the line with her mother's name. "My mother was never married."

He hesitated.

This "complication" went beyond Isabel Poussard being his child bride and standing in the way of him marrying Julianna and receiving her significant dowry and trade support from Aliestle. Isabel might think she was a full-blooded American, but she wasn't. She was also Vernonian, the last of the royal Sachestian bloodline. Her family came from Sachestia, a region in the northern part of the country. She was one of his subjects, one who knew nothing of her parents, her homeland, or her past. Isabel deserved to know the truth, but telling her would be awkward. He wished it were already over.

"Your mother, Evangeline Poussard, was an American college student. She was backpacking through Europe when she met Prince Aleksander Zvonimir." Yesterday, Niko's parents had told him what happened so he could explain it to Isabel. "The two fell in love and eloped."

She looked at Niko as if he'd grown horns. "My mother was married to a prince?"

"Yes."

Isabel's mouth quirked. She appeared as if she was trying not to laugh. "So I suppose next you're going to tell me someone who looks like Julie Andrews is not only my grandmother but also the queen?"

Niko did not understand the reference to the actress. He glanced at Jovan for an explanation.

The Princess Diaries," Jovan explained quietly. "A series of books and movies about an American who discovers she's a princess."

Niko had never heard of any such Princess Diaries, but at least he understood the context. "My mother is the queen. Though being a grandmother would thrill her, I can assure you she looks and sounds nothing like Mary Poppins."

Isabel didn't crack a smile.

So much for his attempt to lighten the mood.

She shook her head. "I don't see how any of this can be true."

"The truth is not always clear."

As she studied the translated document, two lines formed above the bridge of Isabel's nose. He found the trait surprisingly endearing. It made her seem less in control and more open to possibility.

"Let's say my mother was married to this prince, and he's my father," Isabel said. "Why would she give birth to me in America?"

"She didn't. You were born in Vernonia."

"My birth certificate says I was born in the United States. I have a copy." Isabel pursed her lips. "One document is fake. I'm guessing it's yours."

"Yours is the fake," he countered. "Given the political unrest in our country then, I wouldn't be surprised if your parents had another birth certificate made omitting Vernonia and Prince Aleksander's name."

"You sound as if you believe all this." Disbelief dripped from her words. "That Prince Aleksander was my father?"

"Yes," Niko said firmly. "I believe you are Princess Isabel Poussard Zvonimir Kresimir."

She scrunched her nose. "Do I look like a princess?"

"You look like a car mechanic, but that doesn't change the facts. You are a princess of Vernonia and my wife."

Isabel studied the marriage certificate. "Then how did I wind up here?"

"That's what we all want to know," Niko admitted. "My father's staff have been trying to figure that out."

She arched an eyebrow. "Where did they think I was?"

Niko didn't want to answer.

"Where?" she pressed.

"Buried in your family's cemetery."

She gasped. "You thought I was dead?"

"Not me. I was too young to remember, but all of Vernonia believe you were killed with your parents in a car bombing a month after our wedding."

Isabel lowered the papers. "A car bombing?"

"By a splinter faction of Loyalists who were nothing more than terrorists." The way her eyes clouded bothered him. "It was a...troubled time, with two groups aligned to different royal bloodlines. Our marriage was to unite them. But that is in the past now."

The two little lines above the bridge of her nose

returned. Good. Isabel was thinking about what he'd told her. She would see she had to believe—

"I get that you're somebody. Otherwise you wouldn't have the limo, lawyer aide guy, documents, and a police escort. You know my mother's name, but you have the wrong person. The Evangeline Poussard who was my mother never went to Europe. She never married. She wouldn't have married off her baby. And she died due to complications from childbirth, not in a terrorist attack."

"What about the box?" Niko asked.

"I don't know. Maybe there are identical boxes. Yours and hers." Isabel shoved the papers at him. "I don't have time to deal with this. I have work to do."

With her head held high as if she were the Queen of England and not a lowly mechanic, Isabel marched toward the garage.

Niko's fingers crumpled the edges of the papers. He tried to remember the last person besides his father who had dismissed him so readily. "Isabel."

She ignored him.

What an infuriating woman. He wanted to slip into the limousine and forget he'd ever heard the name Isabel Poussard, except he couldn't. They were tied together. Legally. He needed to undo what had been done without their consent. "Wait."

She quickened her step. Most women ran toward him, not away, but he had a feeling Isabel was different from the women he knew.

"Please," he added.

She stopped but didn't turn around.

He forced himself not to clench his jaw. "Before you go, please look at the photograph."

Isabel peered over her shoulder. "What photograph?"

She made him feel more like a peasant than a prince. The phrase "ball and chain" made sense to him if a wife were as strong-willed as Isabel.

He removed the picture from the pouch. "The wedding photo."

She didn't come closer. "I'm on the clock right now. My boss is watching. I can't afford to have my pay docked so you can pull a prank."

"This isn't a prank." The old garage needed a new roof and paint job. Niko wondered if Isabel's financial circumstances were similar to those of her place of employment. "I'll give you one hundred dollars for five minutes of your time."

She straightened. "Seriously?"

Now he had her attention. With the pouch and picture tucked between his arm and side, he removed his wallet, pulled out a hundred-dollar bill, and held it up. "Quite serious."

She hurried toward him.

"You are crazy, but for that kind of money you can have seven minutes." Isabel snatched the money from him and shoved it in her coverall pocket. "Hand over the picture."

Niko gave her the photograph. After examining it so many times during the flight to Charlotte, he had memorized every detail about the twelve people pictured. "You are the baby in the white gown with the tiara. Your mother is holding you. You look like her and there's also a resemblance to your father who is standing to your right. Your paternal grandparents are the two next to him."

Isabel held the photo with both hands. Niko watched her face for some sign of recognition of her mother but saw nothing.

"The quality of the photograph isn't sharp enough to clearly see the faces. And this appears to be from a baptism, not a wedding."

"Only because of the baby." Niko repeated what his mother had told him. "This is a traditional royal wedding pose with the bride and groom in the center and their families on either side."

Isabel narrowed her gaze. "You're the little boy in the suit with the light blue sash across your chest?"

"Yes."

"I don't see a resemblance."

"That was twenty-three years ago."

Isabel traced his boyhood image. "You don't look happy."

Niko wasn't happy right now. He wanted to be rid of this complication, of her. "I imagine a six-year-old boy would not be happy about getting married."

"Who is the other boy?" Isabel asked.

"My older brother."

"Why didn't they marry the baby off to him?" she asked.

Niko noticed Isabel said "the baby" not "me." He took a calming breath to keep his patience under check. "Stefan was the crown prince and betrothed."

She looked up. "Was?"

"My brother was killed during the conflict seven years ago."

Her face grew serious. "I'm sorry for your loss."

Niko didn't want or need her pity, only her cooperation. "All Vernonians suffered losses during the war. I intend to make sure that doesn't happen again. I want to keep the peace and modernize the country."

"Worthy goals." Isabel refocused on the photo. "I'm sorry you came all this way for nothing. My uncle Frank had one picture of my mother that wasn't destroyed when their parents' house burned down. She looked nothing like this."

Niko recalled the dossier containing information about Isabel. She had no living relatives. Her mother had been an only child and orphaned at nineteen following a train derailment that killed her parents. The Zvonimir side of Isabel's family tree had been killed during the conflict. Nowhere in her list of relatives had anyone named Frank appeared.

"Who is Uncle Frank?" Niko asked.

"Frank Miroslav. My mom's older half brother. He

raised me after she died."

Miroslav. Niko recognized the surname, but he did not know how it related to Isabel and her American mother. He glanced at Jovan for clarification.

"The Miroslavs served the Zvonimirs for centuries," Jovan explained. "A deep tie and strong loyalty existed between the two families even though the relationship was master-servant. Franko Miroslav was Prince Aleksander's chauffeur, and I would go as far to say his best friend. Rumors suggest Franko introduced the prince to Evangeline Poussard."

Isabel's mouth dropped open. She closed it.

"That would explain how you escaped out of Vernonia and ended up here," Niko said. "If they used another driver and a doll for the baby after you left the country—"

"No." Her lips tightened. "The woman in the photo is not my mother."

"Are you certain the woman your uncle Frank showed you is your mother?" Niko watched the range of emotions crossing Isabel's face. The vulnerability in her eyes pulled at his heart. "I apologize. This must be difficult for you to hear."

"What you're saying is impossible. Who would let a Vernonian chauffeur into the U.S. with a baby? Where would they get forged American documents?" She studied the photograph as if trying to discover a secret hidden in it. "Uncle Frank wasn't a chauffeur. He wasn't a servant. He was a car mechanic from a small town outside Chicago. The town where he grew up with my mother. His little sister. He was like a father. Why would he lie?"

Niko respected the way she defended the man who raised her. Loyalty to one's family was important and would serve her well. "Perhaps Franko, your uncle Frank, withheld certain truths for your own protection. You were his princess. A faction in Vernonia would have tried to kill you if they'd known you lived."

A faction loyal to Niko's father—even if the king hadn't approved of the group's methods and violence.

Shaking her head, she stared at the photograph. "It's too unbelievable."

Niko would not convince her with words, but perhaps he could show her. "There is a way to find out if what I say is true or not."

Her head jerked up. "How?"

He pulled the chain from beneath his shirt. "We can see if my key fits the lock."

Chapter Four

Please don't fit. Please don't fit. Please don't fit.

The mantra had been running through Izzy's mind for the past thirty minutes, ever since driving home with Boyd and Jovan to retrieve the box from her RV. Now she sat in Rowdy's office with the wooden box on her lap, waiting for the others to join her.

That still doesn't explain why you would give me the box.

Because I am your husband.

Her husband.

Izzy's vision blurred. She felt light-headed.

She clutched the box with its mother-of-pearl inlaid design. She didn't want to drop it on the tile floor. All these years, she'd carted the box around, carefully, but not overly so. The value had been sentimental, not monetary.

Now...

Izzy Poussard, a princess and a crown prince's wife?

No way.

Okay, some women—maybe many women—would be excited to discover they were a long-lost princess from a faraway foreign land and married to a handsome prince. Not Izzy. Oh, sure, she wanted a happily ever after, but her fairy tale didn't involve enchanted castles, sparkling jewelry, and Prince Charming. Her dream revolved around wearing a fire suit in team colors, working over the wall on a pit stop, becoming a crew chief, and standing in the winner's circle with champagne being squirted everywhere.

The door to Rowdy's office opened. Niko, Jovan, Boyd, and her boss entered.

"It'll be a few more minutes, Izzy," Rowdy said. "Duncan Moore is on his way."

"Thanks." Izzy had asked Rowdy to call one of their customers who was a big-name attorney in Charlotte. According to Rowdy, it hadn't taken Duncan five minutes to do an internet search and confirm Niko's identity. A good thing because she needed to talk to a lawyer before Niko and Jovan tried to take the box from her. To her surprise, Niko had offered to cover her legal expenses.

Izzy hadn't wanted to accept the prince's charity. She hadn't relied on anyone since Uncle Frank's death. But she didn't have extra money lying around to cover surprise legal fees. Duncan Moore wasn't only one of the best lawyers in town, he was also the most high-priced. Being prideful was one thing. Being stupid was another.

"And thank you, Niko, for covering my legal expenses," she added.

"You're welcome. I am not here to cause you grief or unwanted expenditures."

Izzy wanted to believe him. The corners of her lips lifted.

He smiled back.

Butterflies flapped in her stomach. *Uh-oh.* She'd better watch herself. Being attracted to a man claiming to be her husband would only complicate things and might lead to her losing ownership of the box.

"Duncan's here," Rowdy announced.

Thank goodness.

Duncan Moore, balding, in his late fifties, and on his third marriage, strutted into the office. On any other man, his polka-dot bow tie would have looked silly with his suit, but the combination worked for the successful attorney.

"Sorry for the delay, everyone. Izzy." Duncan nodded to Rowdy and then to Boyd, who stood against the wall with his arms crossed, looking more like a guard dog than her closest friend. The attorney turned his attention to Niko and bowed. "Your Royal Highness."

Niko acknowledged Duncan with a nod. "This is my aide and lawyer, Jovan Novak."

Jovan shook Duncan's hand.

Unease crept down Izzy's spine. The seriousness of the situation ratcheted up a notch with two lawyers present.

"My paralegal checked out the prince's claims about the marriage while I drove over here," Duncan said. "Vernonia had an old custom of children from royal families marrying but that is illegal now. A groom, however, still presents his wife with a bride box on their wedding night."

Izzy bit her lip. That didn't mean *she* was *his wife*.

"We may proceed now," Niko said.

The tension in the office quadrupled. Izzy's legs shook so much the box jiggled. She placed it on Rowdy's desk and opened the lid. She removed the velvet-covered tray so the keyhole showed. "I didn't realize the tray came out or there was a keyhole until after Uncle Frank died. He allowed me to see the box when I was growing up but never touch it."

"Did your uncle say it belonged to your mother?" Duncan asked.

"No, but I assumed so." Izzy hoped what she said wouldn't give more credence to the prince's claims.

"Uncle Frank told me it was important."

Niko held the key he'd worn around his neck. "Let us see how important."

His hand was as steady as a neurosurgeon's. If it had been her, she would be trembling. Who was she kidding? She *was* trembling.

He inserted the key in the hole.

Izzy was tempted to close her eyes. She held her breath instead. She wanted to know what was inside, but she wanted nothing the prince had told her to be true.

He turned the key.

Click.

"The key fits," Niko announced.

The air whooshed from her lungs.

No, this can't be happening. It can't be true.

The bottom portion slid out. A hidden drawer.

"Would ya look at that," Rowdy said with a hint of awe.

Even though she had been waiting for this moment, she was afraid to look. Her curiosity vanished, replaced by trepidation. She didn't care what was inside. She only wanted things to be the way they'd been before Prince Niko arrived.

"It's the same tiara," Jovan said from across the office.

No. Isabel didn't want to see, so she squeezed her eyes shut. Her chest constricted. She shuddered.

Someone touched her shoulder and squeezed

gently. Rowdy. Both he and Boyd could be big-old teddy bears. She opened her eyes, but Niko's hand was on her.

"Isabel." Concern filled Niko's voice. "Would you rather wait?"

His tenderness brought tears. The situation, not him. Still, she appreciated his gesture of comfort, drew strength from it, too. "No."

Straightening, Izzy peered into the drawer, past the small diamond tiara to find papers, photographs, and more jewelry. Her uncle Frank could have found the box, bought it at a garage sale, or stolen it in desperation. Maybe that was why she had no key.

No, she was being silly now. None of those things would explain Niko knowing her mother's name or his key fitting the lock. Isabel needed to accept what was in front of her, except...

Niko reached into the drawer.

"Wait, sir," Duncan shouted.

The prince froze.

"May I please take a picture of the contents before they are disturbed?" Duncan asked with his cell phone in hand. "I want to document everything. For both Izzy's and your sake."

"Certainly." Niko placed his arm at his side. "I apologize."

The flash of the camera phone reminded Izzy of lightning and intensified the emotions warring inside her. She hated storms. Uncle Frank had died during a lightning storm. She swallowed a tide of grief.

Glancing over her shoulder, she made eye contact with Boyd, who gave her an encouraging smile. He'd always been the strong, silent type, and she was grateful he'd stuck around for the meeting.

Duncan stepped away. "Thank you, sir. Please proceed."

Niko didn't. Instead, he looked at her. "At one time, your parents had a key to the bride box. They placed these contents inside for their daughter. For you. My impatience made me forget my manners. Only you should remove the items."

Anger flared. She loved Uncle Frank, but he'd kept her past a secret. Why? Why hadn't he trusted her? She wanted to know the answer.

"Isabel—"

"I'll do it." She had to find out more. "But only because I need all the facts."

Five people stared at her. She was used to the attention. Few expected a female mechanic to fix their cars. This, however, was different. Unsettling. But Uncle Frank had taught her to hold her head high, no matter how uncertain she might feel inside. If only he were here now...

She scooted her chair closer to the desk. With a shaky hand, she raised the tiara from the box. "It's so tiny."

Niko nodded. "My parents had the tiara commissioned for you to wear at the wedding. The small diamonds represent the towns and villages in the country. The three larger diamonds symbolize you, me, and Vernonia."

"It's impossible to tell if it's the same one in the photo," she said, knowing she was grasping at straws.

"It's the same one," Niko stated confidently.

Izzy set the tiara on the desk. Next, she removed foreign coins and dollar bills, a diamond pendant, an emerald bracelet, and three stunning rings.

Those jewels would be worth a fortune if real. Maybe that was why Niko wanted the box so badly. Money could make people do almost anything.

She picked up a photograph, a picture of a man and a woman.

"Those were your parents," Niko said softly.

Her parents. Izzy wasn't ready to believe it. She focused on the handsome couple. They were smiling and holding hands. They seemed happier than they did in the wedding photograph. "The woman is beautiful."

"You look like her," Rowdy said.

"I wish." Izzy's heart ached for some memory of the two people the prince claimed were her parents.

"You resemble your mother," Niko said. "But you have your father's eyes."

Excitement rushed through her. No one had seen a resemblance between her and Uncle Frank. She removed more photographs. Baby pictures, family portraits, casual snapshots of people she didn't know taken in places she didn't recognize.

Next came an official-looking piece of paper with foreign writing. "I don't know what it says."

"Allow me," Niko offered.

She handed it to him.

He read the document. "It's your birth certificate. Evangeline Poussard Zvonimir is listed as your mother. Aleksander Nicholas Zvonimir is listed as your father. Your place of birth is Sachestia, Vernonia."

Jovan placed the documents they'd shown her earlier on the desk. "In case you are concerned about the translation and wish to compare, ma'am."

"My name is Izzy," she corrected. "I want to see a translation by an impartial person to confirm the document."

"How can you still not believe?" Niko asked.

"I'm being cautious," she admitted. "You've gone to a lot of trouble to find me. You could've offered to buy the box and be done with it. And me."

"You are my wife. I cannot pretend you do not exist and be done with it. Or you."

Izzy grimaced. "Too bad there isn't a birthmark that would prove without a doubt I'm royalty."

"Perhaps there is one." Wicked laughter lit Niko's eyes. "I would be happy to search for it."

Her cheeks warmed.

From the way his face reddened, too, he appeared not to be as unflappable as he led people to believe.

She hadn't been expecting him to blush, but his embarrassment made him seem less a dark, formal prince and more...human. Izzy felt a tad more comfortable with him even if her heart pounded like a piston engine each time he stared at her.

She removed several pieces of paper stapled together. Again, she couldn't read whatever language they were written in. She handed the pages to Niko.

He flipped through them. "This is your father's will, naming you the sole beneficiary of his estate."

"I will need a copy of the will, sir," Duncan said.

"Of course." Niko handed the papers to the lawyer before focusing on Izzy. "Everyone thought you died with your parents so your father's estate went to—"

"You," she said without an ounce of doubt.

"As your husband, your inheritance passed directly to me."

"What kind of estate are we talking about, Your Highness?" Duncan asked.

"What is the approximate net worth?" Niko asked Jovan.

"Approximately twenty-five million euros," his aide replied.

She didn't know much about foreign currency, but a lot of money was at stake. "You're willing to give that to me for a box?"

"The box and an annulment," Niko clarified.

Rowdy whistled. "You won the lottery, Izzy."

Yes. She took a deep breath. That meant it was probably too good to be true.

"Let's not get too excited," Duncan cautioned.

"We have no idea how the legal system works in Vernonia. Each country has its own laws for estates and inheritance. This could be tied up in the court system for years."

"I would never keep anything that rightly belongs to Isabel," Niko stated firmly. "Vernonia might be a small country, but we have a parliamentarian government and a modern justice system. The High Court will not need years to sort this matter out."

"Can't this be taken care of in the U.S.?" Izzy asked.

"Your father's property is in Vernonia," Niko explained. "Besides, the High Court is private. There could be publicity if we used the court here in the United States."

"Duncan?" she asked.

"I know nothing about Vernonia's court system, but Prince Niko is correct about the publicity. America loves royalty. The press would have a field day if they found out you were a Vernonian princess."

Izzy frowned. "I'm not—"

"Come to Vernonia with me," Niko suggested. "We will appear in front of the High Court and have this matter resolved quickly."

Apprehension washed over her. She'd never traveled anywhere. Never flown in an airplane. "I don't have a passport."

"I can pull strings," Niko said.

"Most definitely," Jovan agreed.

She bit her lip. "I don't know. Maybe I should take time to think about it."

"The choice is up to you, Izzy," Duncan said. "I will do what I can from here. I am also happy to fly to Vernonia if you need me there."

At least she wouldn't be on her own, but still…

Silence filled the room. Outside in the garage bay, an air compressor sounded. A horn honked. A car door slammed.

"There's a lot at stake, Izzy," Rowdy said. "Don't let that stubborn streak of yours get in the way."

Stubborn streak? She wasn't stubborn.

"Listen to Rowdy," Duncan advised. "Prince Niko believes you are Princess Isabel. He's willing to give you a multimillion-dollar estate. What more do you need to think about?"

Rowdy and Duncan made good points. Still she hesitated. Cautious. Nervous. Unsure.

Boyd stepped away from the wall. "If Izzy needs time, let her have it."

"Something else is in the drawer, ma'am," Jovan said.

She saw a note-sized envelope tucked away in one corner. *Isabel* was written on the front. The cursive writing looked feminine.

As she picked up the small envelope, her hand trembled. The flap had been tucked inside, not sealed. Carefully, Izzy removed sheets of paper and unfolded the pages. She was happy to see the letter was written in English.

"Our Beloved Daughter." As she read, tears pricked Izzy's eyes. No one had ever called her daughter. Not even Uncle Frank whom she loved like a father.

She continued reading.

You are only a baby yet you are already a bride. Forgive us for sending you to America, but your father sees no other way to keep you safe. Your marriage to Prince Nikola was supposed to protect you and bring peace to Vernonia. But that plan appears to have backfired, and now you are in worse danger. My greatest wish is that you never read this letter. I will destroy it when we arrive in the U.S. If you are reading this note, things didn't go as your father and I hoped. And for that, little princess, I am more sorry than you will ever know.

Your father is torn between the two sides wanting control of Vernonia. The Separatists first wanted to split into their own country, Sachestia, with your grandfather as king. Now they want to wrest full control from King Dmitar and take over the entire country, but your father would rather remain loyal to the throne and Vernonia. Your marriage, however, has unexpectedly antagonized both factions, and made it impossible for him to support either side now. We must leave Vernonia as soon as possible. Your safety is our utmost concern. Once this craziness ends, we will happily return.

We do not dare leave the country together so we are sending you first. We are entrusting you to the care and protection of Franko Miroslav. He is your father's chauffeur, and our dearest and closest friend. He will do whatever is necessary to keep you from harm. We have arranged passage and paperwork so the two of you can escape to the U.S. We will follow the next day.

No one knows of our plan, including the king. He's a good man, but the fewer people who know your whereabouts, the better. Your departure and location will remain a secret until it is safe.

Your father is telling me it's time for you to go. I must sign off now, Isabel.

We love you, our darling Izzy, and hope to be with you soon. Love,

Mommy and Daddy

Izzy took several deep breaths. She'd felt nothing toward the woman in the photo Uncle Frank had shown her, a woman who hadn't been her mother. But this letter written in her mother's own hand provided Izzy with a connection to the woman who gave birth to her. Something she'd longed for since she was little. Something she'd hoped to find by looking for the key.

"True." She slumped in the chair. The girl who was more comfortable with a wrench and in coveralls was a real-life princess. Everything the prince had said... "It's all true."

"I'm sorry," Niko said.

Izzy believed he was. No one wanted to discover they were married to a stranger.

Married.

Her stomach roiled.

Marriage was only part of this. Everything she knew about herself was wrong. Izzy wrapped her arms around her stomach. She wasn't who she thought she was. She had money. A title. A mother and a father.

Izzy recalled her parents' faces from the wedding photograph. A mother and a father who had loved her. A mother and a father who had been killed before she could get to know them.

Emotion clogged Izzy's throat.

But it wasn't too late to fulfill one of their wishes. Her parents had planned on returning to Vernonia when it was safe. That must have meant Uncle Frank planned on going back, too.

Come to Vernonia with me. We will appear in front of the High Court and have this matter resolved quickly.

Maybe seeing the place where she came from would help her figure out who she was and what her future held. She could get the marriage annulled and receive her inheritance. Forget going to pit crew school. She could buy her own racing team.

Izzy rose. "When do you want to leave for Vernonia?"

Chapter Five

When do you want to leave for Vernonia?
Sooner rather than later.

Niko wished they were already there.

Instead, he sat at the table in the recreational vehicle, also known as an RV, according to Jovan, where Isabel lived. His concern over the press discovering the reason behind his unannounced trip to the U.S. continued to grow. But Isabel needed to shower, dress, and pack. They would leave later whether he liked it or not.

Still wearing her bulky, stained coveralls, Isabel

stood in front of the small refrigerator. She rubbed her hands together as if nervous. "Do you want something to drink or eat?"

He appreciated her hospitality. Twenty-three years away from Vernonia hadn't erased centuries of innate good breeding. "No, thank you."

With a hesitant expression, she glanced toward the rear of the RV. "It won't take me more than a few minutes to get ready."

A lump on the faded brown-and-orange plaid cushion behind him made Niko shift positions. "The plane will not take off without us."

As she closed a partition, Niko surveyed the interior with dismay. Warped wood veneer. Cracked cabinet and cupboard doors. Frayed carpeting. Cramped space. The RV had to be older than Isabel.

What had Franko been thinking?

Yes, the chauffeur needed to keep her safe, but why had he never contacted the king for help? Why had Franko allowed her living situation to come to...this?

Niko exhaled a sigh.

Isabel was no damsel in distress. She'd impressed him with the way she'd dealt with her world being turned upside down. His title and money hadn't blinded her. She hadn't accepted the truth without concrete evidence. Surprising, given she lived in near poverty in a shabby RV with no family or resources. A princess of Vernonia deserved better than a life spent working long hours bent over a car engine and coming home to a half-dozen barking, trembling Chihuahuas who lived next door.

She wouldn't be his wife for much longer, but he wanted Isabel to have the life her parents intended for her. She belonged in a castle, to be pampered and protected.

The partition jiggled as if stuck.

"Isabel?" Niko asked, wondering if she needed assistance.

"I'm almost finished." She spoke from behind the thin wall.

He checked his watch. Five minutes. That had to be a world record. Then again, Isabel didn't seem to be a woman who primped or cared much about her appearance.

The partition jerked open.

As she came toward him, he did a double take. All the grease was gone. Isabel's faded blue jeans fit like a second skin, clinging in all the right places, accentuating her feminine curves and long legs. The fabric of her T-shirt stretched across her chest. Her shiny brown hair swung below her shoulders.

Her warm, hazel eyes captivated him. An appealing mix of intelligence and caring shone in their depths.

This was his...wife?

"I'm ready," Isabel announced.

So was he. Niko was ready to follow wherever she wanted to go. He gulped.

"I don't own many clothes." Isabel motioned to

the worn purple duffel bag behind her. The bride box with its original contents was in the limousine with Jovan. "What I have isn't nice enough to wear to court."

"I will make arrangements for you to shop once we arrive." He would head off her financial concerns. "Do not worry about the cost."

"You're already paying for a lot."

"I don't mind." Niko would enjoy seeing her in designer gowns with jewels adorning her graceful neck. "You are my wife."

"Only until the annulment," she reminded him.

"Yes, but until then, taking care of you is my responsibility."

Isabel pushed her chin forward defiantly. "I can take care of myself."

"I know that." He still wouldn't mind a turn. Knowing Isabel didn't want that struck him as odd, but he bowed his head in apology. "A poor choice of words on my part. I promise to make it up to you."

"No need."

As she brushed past him, an appealing mix of vanilla and jasmine tickled his nose. The fragrance was a significant improvement over motor oil. "I want to."

"That's okay." Her smile nearly knocked him off his seat. "I've forgiven you."

Niko didn't want her forgiveness. He wanted...her.

The attraction to Isabel was unexpected and unwelcome. His duties and responsibilities took priority. Niko was practically engaged to Julianna. He shouldn't be attracted to any woman.

Not even your wife?

He balled his hands. His father had taught him to rein in emotions. Otherwise it became a weakness, one that others, particularly adversaries, would use to their advantage.

Niko focused on Isabel's pretty face. "Is there anything else you need to pack for the trip?"

"No. I won't be in Vernonia that long."

"You might enjoy it there."

She shrugged. "This has been my home since I was six."

He couldn't believe she'd lived like this for the past seventeen years. "That's a long time."

"When Uncle Frank bought the RV, he said we would never have to leave home again. We could take it with us." She removed a carton of milk from the refrigerator and poured it down the sink. "I wonder if he was thinking about Vernonia."

"Possibly." Niko surveyed her hovel. "There are other places to live than here."

"I know." Isabel rinsed the carton in the small sink. "This motor home is nothing more than an old metal shed, but I've been happy here. Lonely since Uncle Frank died, but leaving the good memories behind is hard."

"You will make new memories."

"I need to come to peace with the old ones first."

She appeared to stare off into the distance. "So many things about Uncle Frank are making more sense. The lack of photographs. Wanting me to study martial arts. Keeping such a low profile. Being so protective. Even if he wasn't a blood relative, he's family. The only one I ever knew."

Niko nodded. "We shall honor Franko for the sacrifices he made by keeping you safe."

"Thank you." Gratitude shone in her eyes. "Uncle Frank gave up his life in Vernonia to come to America with me, to keep me safe and then take care of me when my parents...couldn't. I believed he was satisfied living here, and I'd be the one to leave someday. Now I know he didn't plan on being in Charlotte forever. He would have returned...home. If that had been a possibility."

One phone call, and Franko and Isabel would have been welcomed back with open arms. But what she said eased some of Niko's concerns about her future. "Your father's estate will enable you to live wherever and however you want."

She sighed. "The thought of having so many choices is intimidating."

"Think of one choice at a time. It won't seem so...overwhelming that way."

"Good advice. Thanks."

Helping her pleased him. "Is there anything else you need?"

"Boyd will check on the RV while I'm away so

everything should be okay."

Niko remembered the tall man who had driven her and Jovan to retrieve the box. The same man had come out to check on her and watched her from the garage. A woman as attractive as Isabel was sure to have men after her. One who worked with her would have an advantage. "Is Boyd your boyfriend?"

"Boyd?" She scrunched her nose. "He's like a brother. Some people think we're a couple, but we're just friends."

The news brought an unfamiliar sense of relief. Except Boyd wasn't the only man in Charlotte. "Do you have a boyfriend?"

"No boyfriend."

"But you date."

"Not nearly as often as I should. I work too much overtime to have a serious relationship. And the boys at the garage can be overprotective when guys drop by."

The news pleased Niko more than it should have.

"What about you?" she asked.

"No boyfriend."

She grinned. "Any girlfriends?"

He'd dated a handful of royals but only casually. Julianna wasn't his girlfriend *per se*, yet she was the woman he planned to marry. Better to keep things simple than give Isabel too complicated an explanation. "Yes, I have a girlfriend."

"What's her name?"

"Julianna. We are planning to marry."

"Congratulations, Niko." Isabel locked a window latch. "I hope the two of you are happy together."

Her enthusiasm surprised him. "You do?"

"Why wouldn't I? I may be your wife, but that was a choice neither of us made, nor would choose today."

Niko winced. He might not choose her, but he didn't see why she wouldn't choose him. He was a prince and a sought-after eligible bachelor according to the tabloids and magazines. "Who would you marry?"

"No one."

"You do not wish to wed?"

"I have things I want to do first."

"Tell me about these things."

"I'm planning to enroll in pit crew school, work on a pit crew, and eventually be a crew chief."

Those were unusual goals for a woman. Unthinkable for a female in Vernonia let alone a princess. "You enjoy racing."

"I love racing. Open-wheel, stock car, go-kart. The vehicle doesn't matter as long as there's a checkered flag at the end."

The passion in her voice reminded him of Julianna when she sailed. Perhaps the two women had more in common than Niko had thought. "Your inheritance will allow you to do what you want in racing."

"Yeah, I guess focusing on going to pit crew school is like a lottery winner who plans to keep their job." Isabel swung the strap of a blue backpack over her shoulder and picked up the purple duffel bag. She opened the door. "Ready to roll, Highness."

Then again, maybe she didn't have that much in common with Princess Julianna after all.

Chapter Six

Across the tarmac at the Charlotte Douglas International Airport, jet engines roared.

Unreal.

Izzy stood on the landing at the top of the portable aircraft staircase with a gorgeous prince who was her husband. She couldn't believe what was happening.

Each beat of her heart slammed against her ribs. She'd never dreamed of traveling to a far-off destination except to attend a race. But here she was about to board a private plane and fly to another continent...

An airplane sped down the runway.

She shivered. Soon that would be her plane. Well, his.

Some might call traveling to Vernonia an exciting adventure. Not Izzy. Her misgivings kept increasing by the minute. Maybe she should have asked Duncan to come with her. Or Boyd. Both had offered, but she didn't want to be a burden.

Another aircraft taxied by. The silver, red, and blue color scheme seemed festive compared to Vernonia's solid white airplane with only aircraft numbers, letters, and a small coat of arms for markings.

A royal coat of arms.

A chill ran along her spine.

Never in a million years could she have imagined this happening to anyone, let alone her. A grease monkey who cared more about the Cup Series standings than the lines of succession for European thrones was now a princess?

Unbelievable.

Or, thinking about one of her favorite movies that featured a princess, would that be inconceivable?

At the bottom of the stairs, a security detail stood watch. A customs agent checked paperwork with the uniformed liaison officer who appeared to be part of the flight crew.

The shock of discovery still had her reeling. Denial battled acceptance. Despite the physical evidence, Izzy found the truth difficult to accept. Impossible, really.

Would she ever feel like Princess Isabel Poussard Zvonimir Kresimir?

Izzy doubted it.

Facing the open doorway, Izzy sensed rather than felt Niko standing behind her. She clutched the strap of her purple duffel bag and adjusted her blue backpack.

"It's time to board." His warm breath fanned her neck.

Awareness shot through Izzy. Her uneasiness quadrupled.

Hold it together.

She straightened, not wanting to appear weak. Uncle Frank had taught her to be tough. She didn't want to let him down. "I know."

Yet the open doorway loomed in front of her like a mysterious black hole. Her heart pounded so fast Izzy thought her chest might explode.

Breathe.

She did.

All she had to do was cross the threshold and board the plane. Too bad her shoes felt as if someone had glued the soles to the staircase's platform. They seemed to know what Izzy kept trying to forget.

This wasn't only about flying jitters. She had no idea what awaited her on the other side of the plane's doorway or when she arrived in Vernonia.

That terrified her.

She'd never faced the unknown alone. Uncle Frank

had been gone for five years, but before that he'd paved the way. Even after his death, she'd continued working at Rowdy's, living in the RV, and following the plan they'd dreamed up together. Her routine hadn't changed except now she cooked for one, not two. Today, she found herself on a new, uncertain path with her seemingly safer plans swept away. Nothing would be the same.

Worse, there was no turning back.

Izzy blew out a breath.

Her life was irrevocably changed whether she boarded the plane or stayed in Charlotte. The realization made her light-headed. She swayed.

The prince moved closer, crowding her from behind. He emanated strength and warmth and something one-hundred-percent male.

Her pulse skittered.

Uh-oh. Izzy needed to put distance between them. Not that she had room to go anywhere. She shifted to the side until her hip hit the staircase railing. "Give me a minute."

Niko gently placed his hand on the curve of her back.

Izzy stiffened. The slight touch added to her apprehension.

"You will have plenty of time once we board," he said. "We won't take off immediately."

It didn't matter. She was losing control of the situation, of her life. "Things are happening too fast. I need everything to slow down."

"That will happen when we are in the air. We have a long flight ahead of us."

One that would carry her away from everything familiar. Nerves smacked into her like a rogue wave. Her stomach clenched.

"Your Highnesses?" Jovan said.

"Go ahead of us," Niko answered him. Jovan appraised Izzy before stepping onto the plane.

"Isabel," Niko said.

Another plane took off. The roar louder than any engine she'd heard at the racetrack. Goose bumps prickled her skin.

"I told you I need a minute." She spoke harsher than she intended.

"It's been an eventful day."

His calm voice irritated her. He acted too unaffected by all this.

"You think?" She swallowed around the crown-jewel-sized lump in her throat. "I doubt anyone else has had a day like today. I wish it were all a dream. But it's not. And now I'm stuck."

"Stuck?"

"Having to travel to Vernonia to annul the marriage and get my inheritance," she admitted. "Unfortunately, I have no idea what will happen once we arrive. I may have been born there, but it might as well be Mars."

Niko's assessing appraisal made her feel like one of

Cinderella's ugly stepsisters, but she fought the urge to hunch her shoulders and hide.

"Vernonia is different from the United States," he admitted. "Some would call our country old-fashioned. Others, antiquated. Especially regarding gender roles."

Not our country. His.

Izzy half laughed with a mix of desperation and fear. "If you're trying to make me feel better, it's not working."

"I will not lie to you, Isabel." He didn't sound upset at her, but his tone lacked the compassion he'd shown her earlier. "Your life has changed. But you will not have to deal with any of this on your own."

A sense of inadequacy swept through her. Izzy was used to handling everything on her own, but she was completely out of her comfort zone here and shaking in her held-together-with-duct-tape tennis shoes.

"It will be my pleasure to help you," he offered.

Niko made a dashing knight in shining armor, but Izzy didn't appreciate being cast in the role of a damsel in distress. She didn't want or need his help. "Thanks, but I can do this on my own."

Please let me be able to do this on my own.

With a deep breath, Izzy stepped through the doorway and onto the plane.

"Welcome aboard, Your Royal Highness," a male flight attendant with a crew cut and navy blue uniform greeted. "We have a seven-course dinner for you and movies for your entertainment."

It took Izzy a minute to realize the man was addressing her.

"Thank you," she muttered, wondering how he knew who she was.

The flight attendant smiled. "Would you like me to escort you to your seat, ma'am?"

"Thank you, Luka, but I will show Princess Isabel the way," Niko said before Izzy could answer.

Luka bowed. "Enjoy your flight, ma'am, sir."

"I thought you wanted to keep my identity a secret to avoid publicity," she whispered to Niko.

"Only until we appear before the High Court," he explained quietly.

As his male scent surrounded her, heat rushed through her veins. She hoped the High Court would be their first stop after they landed.

"Do not worry," he continued. "The crew is part of the Vernonian Air Force. I trust them with the information. As I do the palace staff."

A lot of people seemed to know about her, but he was the prince. "If you say so."

"I do."

Holding her backpack in front of her, Izzy made her way along the aisle. The interior, a mix of warm beiges, browns, and blues, created a welcoming environment. Couches and tables filled the first section of the cabin.

"This is the lounge area," Niko explained. "Come here if you want to stretch your legs."

"I doubt I'll unfasten my seat belt during the flight."

The corners of his mouth lifted. "That may get uncomfortable if you have to use the facilities."

Her cheeks warmed. She hadn't considered needing the bathroom.

Wide, luxurious leather seats filled the next section. Nothing like the narrow, cramped, and squished-together ones her high school classmates had described after their graduation trip to the Caribbean. Izzy hadn't been able to afford to go, so she'd stayed home and worked at Rowdy's garage.

Times sure had changed since then. Mechanic Izzy Poussard was now Princess Isabel, the wife of the crown prince of Vernonia. She nearly laughed at the absurdity.

"This is where we sit for takeoff and landing, or, if you choose," Niko said, "the entire flight."

Izzy passed the row where Jovan sat. People she hadn't seen before filled other seats. She continued to the last row of empty seats in front of a divider.

Before she could sit, a female flight attendant rushed from the rear of the aircraft. The young woman wore a navy jacket and skirt. Her blond hair was neatly braided into a bun. "Good evening. Allow me to hold your backpack, Your Royal Highness."

Before Izzy could speak, the attendant lifted the strap out of her hand.

Every one of her muscles tensed, bunching into

tight balls. She wasn't used to being catered to, nor did she feel like royalty.

She sat in the window seat and buckled her seat belt.

The flight attendant handed her the backpack. "Would you care for something to drink or eat, ma'am?"

"No, thanks." Izzy's stomach was doing cartwheels so a drink or food wouldn't be a smart idea. Her nerves threatened to get the best of her. Over the flight, over Vernonia, over Niko. Maybe if she distracted herself...

She pressed a button. The overhead light illuminated. She twisted a knob. Air flowed through the nozzle.

Niko sat next to her. "Are you certain you do not want anything?"

Izzy wanted this to be over with, but that would not happen tonight or tomorrow. Soon, she hoped. "No, thanks, Your Highness."

"Call me Niko."

"I'd rather not get in the habit of calling you by your first name. Once our marriage is annulled, you won't want to be on such familiar terms with a commoner."

"You are not a commoner." His voice was tight. "You are a princess by birth. Royal Sachestian blood flows through your veins."

"That may be true, but I was raised an American. Royalty is something other countries have."

"Americans have unofficial royalty. The Kennedys and the Rockefellers come to mind."

"I suppose we do, but I never aspired to be a princess beyond the age of four or five. Wearing a tiara and sparkly gown has never been a dream of mine."

"You may be an American, but you are a Vernonian, too." He spoke as if her being from his country meant everything. No one had ever spoken to her that way. Not even Uncle Frank. "The history of your family will amaze you. Make you proud."

Intrigued, she leaned toward him. "I have a family history?"

"Your lineage can be traced for centuries. Your father's family played an integral role in the formation of our country, when Sachestia in the north merged with the south to form what we now call Vernonia." He fastened his seat belt. "If you have questions about anything, please ask."

"I—" The lights in the cabin flickered. She clutched the seat armrests until her knuckles went white. "What's that?"

"The APU, auxiliary power unit, coming on," he explained. "It powers the lights and air system while we are in flight."

"Oh, yeah. I should have remembered that."

The plane moved backward.

Oh boy, oh boy, oh boy.

"Do not worry." Niko covered her hand with his large one. His was warm but not soft. Scars and calluses covered his skin. "The aircraft is being moved so the pilot can taxi to the runway."

Forget about the plane. His touch disturbed her more than it comforted. She tried to slip her hand from beneath his but couldn't. "I'm sorry if I've been acting like a wimp, but I'm okay now."

"You've handled the situation remarkably well, Isabel. You should be proud of yourself."

She sat taller. She wanted to be brave for him but mostly herself. Uncle Frank would have wanted her to be that, too.

The engines roared to life. She sucked in a breath. *Nothing to worry about. Nothing to worry about.*

The phrase became her mantra.

The plane taxied to the runway. Out the window, the airport lights shined in the darkness. Pretty, but she would rather be at home alone than sitting on a luxurious private jet holding hands with a handsome prince.

Too late to back out now.

Izzy pressed her feet against the floor.

"We will be in the air shortly," Niko said.

All she could do was nod.

The jet lurched to a stop. The engines whined, the sound growing louder. She was too nervous to appreciate the speed of the rotor. The cabin shook like the crowd at Daytona when cars went three wide. Izzy held her breath.

Suddenly, the jet speeded down the runway.

She glanced out the window at the world passing by her.

"Remember to breathe," he said.

She did.

Niko squeezed her hand.

This time, his touch reassured her. His mouth drew her attention. She thought about kissing him to take her mind off flying for the first time, but that seemed extreme. Maybe burying her face against his chest until this was over would be better. She closed her eyes instead.

"Look at me, Isabel."

She forced her eyes open.

"You are safe," he said. "As long as you are with me, you will always be safe."

His confidence and strength made her almost believe him. But safe didn't exist. Not really. If it did, her parents would be alive. Uncle Frank, too.

The vibrations increased until Izzy thought the plane might break apart. The forward momentum pushed her against her seat. Niko laced his fingers with hers.

The aircraft lifted off the ground.

The lights below grew smaller and smaller until they disappeared altogether. The aircraft climbed at a steep angle, as if it were a fighter jet, not a passenger plane.

The interior jolted.

She sucked in another breath.

"A patch of turbulence," Niko explained. "Normal."

None of this was normal. Not the takeoff. Not the prince sitting next to her. And not this life-altering adventure she was embarking upon.

After what seemed like forever, the plane leveled.

"We've reached cruising altitude." Niko kept his hand on hers. "Not too bad."

It wasn't a question.

"No," she admitted. "But we still have to land."

The corners of his mouth lifted. "Landing will be easier."

She found that impossible to believe. "Seriously?"

He nodded. "The time change will tire you. You may be asleep when the wheels touch ground."

"I'm not sure I'll be sleeping after everything that's gone on. My mind's a jumble right now."

"You should try to rest," he encouraged her. "Tomorrow will be a big day."

"Are we going straight to the court?" she asked.

"The High Court is not in session on Saturday. We will go to the castle."

"Castle?"

"My parents want to meet you."

Her body tensed. "I've never met a king or a queen."

"You have, but you don't remember."

"What's your father like?" Izzy asked.

"He's very...kingly."

"That's intimidating," she admitted. "I'm glad I don't remember meeting him or I might be more nervous than I am."

"He only wants to reassure himself you are alive and well." Niko squeezed her hand. "You have nothing to worry about."

The prince was wrong. Dead wrong.

She had lots to worry about, starting with the tingles shooting up her arm as he touched her. Worse was the realization she didn't want him to let go of her hand.

Not now.

Not when they landed in Vernonia.

Not...ever.

Chapter Seven

As the plane cruised at thirty-three thousand feet, the interior cabin lights dimmed. The engines droned, but unlike the white noise device Niko traveled with, the sound did not soothe him. With so many things weighing on his mind, sleep eluded him. But a busy day lay ahead. He should try to relax.

Niko pressed the button on the armrest. The leather seat reclined into a more comfortable position, but a continuous stream of information flowed through his brain. Thoughts about Vernonia, Julianna, his father, and most especially the woman sitting in the seat next to him.

Isabel.

He angled toward her.

She sat with her seat reclined and her head resting against a pillow. She'd fallen asleep after struggling against her heavy, drooping eyelids and drawn-out yawns for almost an hour.

Isabel's unwillingness to surrender to her tiredness without a fight made him wonder if she turned everything into a battle. Her actions today suggested as much, but reining in that tendency would be worth the effort because her lineage would bring a political peace to the country.

The fighter in Isabel likely arose from the Vernonian in her. Niko nearly laughed because she would probably disagree with him. No matter, he would want her on his side. If he had a side. Thankfully, those days were over. No one would be forced to choose who to support or who to fight again.

No one would die.

That was what Stefan would have wanted.

A united Vernonia was his father's goal and had been Stefan's as well. Now, it was Niko's.

Once he and Julianna said "I do," he would have the financial resources and international support to put the war behind them and bring his country into the modern age.

Nothing could stand in his way.

Not an antiquated custom. Not a childhood bride.

Niko focused on Isabel once again.

He'd been married to her for the past twenty-three years, almost her entire life and over three-quarters of his. If not for the missing bride box, he would have never known she existed. Things would have been less complicated for him, but once she received her inheritance, her circumstance would improve dramatically. A better life awaited Isabel. One her parents would have wanted for her. That pleased him and made what he was going through more acceptable.

Yet he worried what responsibilities would be thrust upon Isabel's shoulders after she arrived in Vernonia. People would judge her. She needed training to be a proper princess. Stylish clothes and makeup lessons would improve her appearance. A manicure would help with her dirty, chipped nails though not much could rid her hands of the calluses, cuts, and scars. Perhaps she could start a new fashion trend by wearing gloves.

He wanted her transition to be smooth, not fueled with doubts and disparaging remarks. Those would make things difficult on Isabel. The less criticism and critique, the better.

Despite her disregard for etiquette and style, she was a refreshing change from other royals he'd encountered. She was not caught up in the tangled web of tradition. Even Julianna, as perfect as she was, came from a kingdom more out-of-date and behind-the-times than Vernonia.

He might not understand Isabel's passion, but he admired her for working on cars. He remembered his time as a soldier. Living day to day, sometimes hour to hour. His military service during the civil war had given him a taste of an ordinary existence. Even after she left her mechanic days behind her, she could relate to the people at their level.

That would be a huge positive for their country.

Isabel might not know how to be a princess, but she was a contemporary woman, something rarely found in Vernonia. As he moved forward with his plans, he could use that to his advantage.

A cashmere blanket was tucked around her shoulders. The cover rose and fell with each of her breaths. Her hair fanned across the pillow, the brown strands contrasting with the white fabric. The slender column of her neck contradicted the stiff backbone she'd shown earlier. The lack of makeup and lip gloss didn't diminish the curve of her cheek and fullness of her lips. She possessed a natural beauty.

Although Niko appreciated her spirit and self-reliance, her softer side appealed to him as much or more. The defiant set of her chin and tight jaw had relaxed. She appeared peaceful and serene. A way she didn't look when awake.

Her slightly parted lips seemed to smile. The result of a pleasant dream? A dream about him?

Not likely. Besides, her dreams were none of his business. Nor did he belong in them even if he found her...more attractive than he'd expected.

Isabel might be his wife, but he should think of her as a sister. Anything else would be inappropriate given his intention to marry Julianna.

Isabel shifted in her seat. She stretched like one of the feral cats living in the stable. As she settled into a new position, the top half of her blanket fell from her shoulders and pooled on her lap.

Niko pulled up the blanket and tucked the edges around her shoulders.

"Sir." Jovan stood in the aisle.

Niko jerked his hands away from Isabel, feeling as if the palace's renowned pastry chef had caught him sneaking a *tulumbe* from a batch soaking in syrup overnight.

"It is late." Jovan handed him a blanket. "Nothing more can be accomplished until we arrive in Vernonia. Please rest, sir."

Sleep was futile, but Niko placed the blanket on his lap. Jovan was only doing his job. "The shopping arrangements..."

"Have been taken care of, sir. Princess Julianna has offered her help and expertise."

The future wife helping the soon-to-be former one. The thought of the two women, so very different, spending time together made Niko's temples throb. "That will be...interesting."

"Princess Julianna's sense of duty is matched only by your own. She wants to help you, sir."

Niko hoped Isabel accepted the help. That independent streak of hers might get in the way. "Julianna will make a fine queen."

Jovan nodded. "She will also be an excellent role model for Princess Isabel to emulate, sir."

"Yes." Niko lowered his voice to keep from waking Isabel. "She will need all the advice and help Julianna can offer."

Jovan smiled at the sleeping woman. "The princess is not what I expected, but she has...spirit. She puts on no airs. Plays no games."

"She has a down-to-earth charm," Niko agreed. "In time, she could become a role model herself."

Jovan's brows furrowed. "I do not believe she intends to stay long enough for that to happen, sir."

"Once Isabel sees what Vernonia has to offer, she will stay. We can have her things packed and shipped."

"You sound certain, sir."

"I am," Niko stated. "You saw the dump she calls home. Her life in the United States leaves much to be desired."

"She doesn't seem to mind that life, sir. And with her inheritance..."

"Perhaps she does not know any better."

Isabel's full lips still appeared to be smiling. He wouldn't mind a taste. A kiss.

No. He couldn't allow himself to go there even if he was...tempted.

His gaze kept wanting to stray to the woman next

to him, but he remained focused on his aide. "Staying in Vernonia is best for Isabel."

She deserved all life offered, not struggling to make ends meet and living in an old, metal box with wheels.

"I wonder what Princess Isabel will say about that, sir," Jovan said.

"She may not have an Ivy League education, but she is intelligent." Niko wanted to get to know her better and see how she best fit into Vernonia. "It won't take her long to realize where her future lies."

"If she disagrees, I suppose we can finally make use of the tower, sir," Jovan joked.

Niko laughed. "You've been spending too much time around my father. But I suggest you don't mention the tower to Isabel."

Her stubborn streak and American idealism might be offended even if the tower hadn't been used for its original purpose in centuries. He wanted her to feel comfortable and welcome, not be afraid or offended by the country of her birth.

Because whether she realized it or not, Vernonia was and always would be her home.

"Isabel."

A man called Izzy's name, but she didn't want to wake up. Her alarm clock hadn't buzzed. That must mean this was part of her dream, an odd mix of a fairy tale and a nightmare featuring a brooding, handsome prince holding her captive in a tower.

"Isabel," the man said again.

Her name rolled off his tongue in three syllables. I-sa-bel. She liked the way it sounded. Snuggling against the pillow, she wanted more sleep and more of him calling for her.

The bed lurched as if she were riding on a flying carpet that had come to a sudden stop.

"Welcome to Vernonia," the male voice continued.

Where?

And then she realized.

Izzy wasn't asleep, dreaming in her bed. She forced her heavy eyelids open. Bright sunlight streamed through the small window to her right.

She blinked. The plane had not only landed but also parked. A small turboprop taxied by.

Every single muscle tensed. Yesterday had been real. The box. Her parents. The prince.

She clutched the armrests.

"Good morning, Isabel," Niko said from the seat next to her.

Izzy saw nothing good about today. She was tired, surrounded by strangers, and far away from home. She turned toward Niko to tell him as much, but her mouth went dry.

Hello, Prince Hottie.

Heat pulsed through her veins.

The stubble on Niko's face gave him a sexier,

dangerous edge. Especially with his scar. A real bad boy. His clothes remained unwrinkled, as if he'd just finished a photo shoot, not spent the night flying across an ocean and a continent.

"You didn't eat much dinner last night," he said. "Are you hungry?"

She wouldn't mind a bite of him.

Strike that. A serving of prince sunny side up wasn't on the menu this morning. Or anytime. This wasn't some guy. He was her husband. At least until the High Court was in session on Monday.

Izzy toyed with the blanket covering her lap. "No, thanks. I'm not hungry."

"I shall have a meal delivered to your room in case you want to eat later."

Room service? She wiggled her toes with anticipation. She'd never stayed at a hotel. Maybe this trip would have a few bright spots. "Thanks, but please don't go to any trouble. I can order when I'm ready."

"It is no trouble."

But it was for her. "I prefer to do things myself."

"Luka came by with the warm towels," Niko continued as if she hadn't spoken. "If you want one—"

"No, thanks. I'm good."

Tired though. Izzy yawned, hoping doing so wouldn't break princess protocol. She needed more sleep. A shower wouldn't hurt. Once she arrived at the hotel...

"Ready to see your homeland?" Niko asked.

Vernonia might be her place of birth, but she would never call the country home. She was an American as red, white, and blue as the flag. "I suppose I can't stay on the plane all day."

"You could."

"Really?"

"You're a princess." He spoke as if she knew the rules about being royalty. "But you might get bored."

"I don't do well being bored."

"That doesn't surprise me."

Standing, she placed the straps of her backpack over her shoulders.

"The crew will carry your pack," Niko said.

"I don't mind."

"Serving you is an honor."

"I'm, uh, not comfortable with that. My wallet and ID are inside."

"A princess hauling her own bag will appear odd."

"It's my purse," she countered. "Besides, I don't care what other people think of me."

A muscle flicked at his jaw. "You've made that quite obvious."

Niko pressed his lips together. The same way he'd done when they were in Charlotte. He wasn't pleased with her. Too bad. He'd better get used to how she acted because they were stuck together until the High Court declared otherwise.

"Just so you know." She tilted her chin. "People

telling me what I can or can't do bug me."

She walked down the aisle before he could say anything else to annoy her.

The other passengers, who had been introduced by job titles not names, had deplaned. The flight crew, including the pilots, stood in a line outside the cockpit. Izzy thanked each and exited.

At the top of the portable staircase, she took a deep breath. The crisp air refreshed her.

The airport was smaller than the one in Charlotte and seemed to be built on a plateau. Everything from the control tower to the runways appeared brand new. Beyond the runways, the flat landscape gave way to foothills that led to rocky mountains.

Niko joined her on the landing. He motioned to a black limousine at the bottom of the stairs. "Our chariot awaits."

Attached to the front of the car were two small blue and white flags with yellow emblems in the center, fluttering in the cool breeze. Uniformed guards with large guns stood nearby. A man in a black suit unloaded the luggage from a cart. He carefully placed her battered duffel bag into the trunk as if it contained fragile Faberge eggs, not thrift store bargain buys.

As feelings of inadequacy swept through her, Izzy clutched the metal handrail like a lifeline. She was out of her league here.

Niko extended his arm. "I'm only offering my assistance because you must be tired."

His gesture of chivalry brought tears to her eyes. Uncle Frank used to do the same thing before escorting her across the street or down a parking lot staircase. Izzy wiped her face.

Boy, she must be jet-lagged to get so sentimental. But Niko was right. Her legs were stiff from the flight. Her shoes fit tighter, making her wonder if her feet had swollen. She couldn't pretend she wasn't feeling more exhausted by the minute.

Falling down the stairs was a distinct possibility in her current condition and wouldn't be a good start to her visit to Vernonia. Forget making a *faux pas*. The stage was set for an epic failure. She couldn't allow that to happen.

Better safe than sorry. Izzy wrapped her arm around Niko's. "Thanks."

Together, they descended the stairs. He went slowly, shortening his stride. For her sake, Izzy realized. Her thoughts about him being a knight in shining armor weren't too far off. Still, she wasn't comfortable needing his help. She'd been on her own for the last five years. Leaning on someone else felt unnatural even if it was only for the length of the portable staircase.

"You are not merely tired." A slight breeze ruffled the ends of his hair. Even the scar on his face suited him. He wasn't a perfect prince, but he wasn't *that* bad. "You are exhausted."

"Yeah." She struggled not to yawn. "Though I'm not sure why since I slept most of the flight."

"Jet lag. It's the middle of the night in Charlotte," he explained. "You need time to adjust. You can rest soon. Though not for too long or you will throw your body clock off more."

"A short nap is all I need."

"A short nap you shall have." He grinned.

Her breath caught in her throat. Izzy wouldn't mind if he tucked her in and kissed her goodnight.

Her foot missed a step. As if in slow motion, she fell. Her right hand clutched the railing. Her left hand gripped Niko's arm. Somehow he caught her.

"Are you okay?" he asked.

His strong arms righted her so she stood upright.

"Yes," she said grateful. "Thanks to you."

"Only a few more steps."

Thank goodness. Her body trembled. Not because of the near fall but because of Niko. His compelling presence drew her in like a tow truck's winch. She needed to put some distance between them.

As soon as Izzy reached the tarmac, she slid her arm from his. The chauffeur opened the rear door. She climbed inside. Leaning against the leather seat, she stretched out her legs, relieved not to be next to Niko.

He slid into the limousine and sat next to her even though the rest of the seats were empty.

She blew out a breath. Didn't he understand the concept of personal space?

His thigh pressed against hers. Not on purpose, yet her temperature rose.

The prince might be a hottie, but he was off-limits. He was her husband, but he planned on marrying someone else. She couldn't allow herself to be attracted to him.

Izzy scooted away to defuse her growing awareness of him. "Where's Jovan?"

"Next to the driver." Niko pressed a button and lowered the dark glass separating them from the front of the limousine. "Jovan is confirming everything will be ready for you to shop today."

"I don't have to go shopping today."

"I know you are tired. I wish you had more time to adjust, but my parents expect you at dinner tonight."

"Tonight?" Izzy's voice cracked. "That's, um, nice of them, but dinner isn't necessary. I mean, in a few days, we won't be married."

"Our parents were friends. They orchestrated our wedding," Niko explained. "You are and always will be a princess of Vernonia and should consider us family."

Family.

Izzy felt a pang in her heart.

The word stirred strange emotions. Ones she'd tried to ignore while growing up. She'd had no family except Uncle Frank. "That's a generous offer, but I feel more like a serf than a royal."

"A royal serf. An oxymoron."

"How about a royal waif?" she suggested.

Laughter danced in his warm eyes. "Serf, waif, or princess, you'll find acceptance here, Isabel."

The only people who had accepted her were at Rowdy's garage, but she appreciated Niko trying to make her feel better. She stifled a yawn.

"After you rest, you will shop. Someone will help you select and organize the various outfits you'll need."

"Um, thanks." Izzy didn't know whether to be offended or grateful he was providing her help. She wasn't colorblind, but she didn't care about what was in style. "I don't need a lot."

"Most women enjoy having several outfits."

"I'm not like other women."

His gaze raked over her. "No, you are not."

That didn't seem to be a compliment, but she wasn't offended. What he said reaffirmed what she knew in her heart. Izzy Poussard wasn't princess material. She didn't belong in Vernonia. She needed to take care of business, learn about her family, and return home to Charlotte. ASAP.

As the limo left the airport, Niko pointed out the window toward a town they approached. "We're entering the capital city."

The city was smaller and more compact than Charlotte, with narrower roads, but the commotion on the streets suggested a busy, bustling town. A crane lifted steel girders while men in yellow hard hats guided them onto the fourth floor of a construction site. Next door, scaffolding covered the front of a new office building and men painted. Across the street, a woman in a multicolored skirt, boots, and a long sweater pushed a baby stroller. Two teenagers kicked a soccer ball as they hurried past the woman and child. A man in a business suit entered a newer five-story building made of steel and glass.

"What do you think?" Niko asked.

"I didn't expect a modern city in a country that allows children to marry."

"I told you, that is against the law now."

"Yes, you did." She saw no garbage or graffiti. That was quite an achievement. "Everything is so new and clean. Even the streets."

"Bombing demolished this area," he explained. "Rebuilding takes time and money. Projects are being spread out to best utilize our resources."

The limousine drove into another part of town. This section consisted of smaller stone and brick rectangular buildings each painted a different color. Some were new. Many were older. Several had window boxes but no flowers. "Is this a residential area?"

"Yes."

Izzy noticed one similarity among the colorful homes. Holes on almost every structure. Bullet pocks?

A memorial sign hung on a pole. Flowers and pictures were attached. She shuddered.

"I can't imagine what living through a war must be like. Just watching the television coverage of one is difficult, but this..." A weight pressed against her chest. "I hope the country never experiences that again."

"It won't," Niko stated firmly. "War is never

pleasant, but fighting amongst your own is brutal. Friend against friend. Brother against brother. Both the Loyalists and the Separatists accepted the treaty unanimously. Our post-conflict elections have gone well. We are fortunate to have not faced the problems that plagued other Balkan countries. I am determined to see peace upheld and good triumph for all Vernonians. No matter what side they supported in the conflict."

Her respect for him grew. "Good luck."

"Thank you."

The limousine left the town and traveled up a steep hill. Tall trees lined both sides of the road and cast shadows on the pavement. As the car crested a ridge, a castle appeared in the distance.

Her heart beat in triple time.

A fairy-tale castle, so perfect it appeared to have been painted on a canvas of blue. Turrets jutted into the sky. Leaded glass windows sparkled. Silver roof tiles gleamed beneath the morning sun. She'd never seen anything so beautiful in her life.

"Wow."

"We are fortunate the castle remained in such good shape given the battles fought in the area. The wall took several mortar hits, but that was the worst of the damage."

"Thank goodness." Jovan glanced over his shoulder. "The royal family stayed in residence during the conflict."

"When we weren't fighting."

Hearing a royal would be on the front line surprised Izzy. "You fought in the war?"

"Yes." Niko's one word spoke volumes. "My father, Stefan, and I fought with the Loyalists to preserve the boundaries and traditions of all people."

Izzy could imagine Niko as a warrior, fierce and hard, defending his people to the death. That took courage and strength. She pointed to the jagged scar on his cheek. "Did you get that fighting?"

"Yes, we are all marked by the conflict. Some scars are visible. Others are not."

Did Niko have other scars? Hidden ones?

Izzy wanted to know, but she didn't know him well enough to ask. Still, she would like to see if there was more to this seemingly in-control prince than met the eye.

Curiosity about the man her parents had married her off to. Nothing else.

As the limousine approached the castle, the immense structure loomed in front of her. Was that a moat?

She peered out the window.

Yes, it was. A river flowed underneath a bridge flanked by armed guards. One waved them across.

Two minutes later, the car stopped in front of tall, wooden doors. A uniformed man stepped outside. His white dress shirt, creased pants, and sharp jacket made Izzy feel under-dressed in her faded jeans, T-shirt, and ratty sneakers. No wonder the prince was so keen on her shopping.

"Your bag will be delivered to your room, ma'am," Jovan said before exiting the limousine.

"Wait a minute." A sudden coldness settled at her core. "I thought I was staying at a hotel."

"You are legally my wife. You will stay at the castle until the annulment has been granted."

"I want to stay at a hotel."

"No."

Ugh. He hadn't listened to her. If he had, he wouldn't be telling her what to do. "But—"

"The castle is the most suitable place for you to stay."

Izzy could rattle off a hundred reasons why she shouldn't stay here with him, the queen, and the king. She settled on one. "I'd be more comfortable in a hotel."

"You will be more comfortable here," Niko countered. "The castle's staff will cater to your every whim."

"I don't have any whims that need catering."

He set his jaw. "No hotel."

Her eyelids felt heavy. She needed to sit down. "I really—"

"This isn't up for negotiation."

Her tiredness put her at a disadvantage. She couldn't think fast enough. "Please."

"You will sleep better here than anywhere. Trust

me."

Izzy didn't trust him. She couldn't. He was a stranger.

"It's also safer for you to stay at the castle for security reasons," he added.

Okay, that she could accept.

"Fine. I'll concede on that point." She stared down her nose. "But just so you know, as soon as we get the annulment, I'm outta here."

Chapter Eight

I'm outta here.

Niko had one parting thought before handing Isabel off to a maid named Mare.

Good riddance.

He was trying to help Isabel, ease her into a new way of life in Vernonia, but her self-reliance was a Mount Everest-sized obstacle. She had no idea how a royal was supposed to act, and starting from scratch would not be easy. A month locked in the tower with only etiquette lessons and protocol books might help her learn to be a princess, but even then she might need more time.

As he strode through the hall, the sharp click from his heels against the wood floor echoed his irritation.

"Niko."

Stopping, he flexed his fingers. He did not want his annoyance at his "wife" to affect his soon-to-be bride.

Julianna stood in the library doorway. Her designer skirt and short jacket complemented her figure the same way her deftly applied makeup accentuated her facial features. Her long, blond hair with golden highlights gleamed under the lights. "Welcome home."

As he stared at her, one word came to mind—perfection. He couldn't have found a better princess to be Vernonia's future queen. Her beauty matched her intelligence. She spoke German, French, Spanish, and English fluently. It wouldn't take her long to learn his country's language. She was a world-class-caliber sailor and an excellent spokesperson. She not only had family connections and wealth, but her sense of duty also set her above the unmarried royals he'd met. She understood what her country expected of her, and she fulfilled her duty without question. One hundred and eighty degrees different from Isabel.

"It's good to see you, Julianna."

"And you." She sounded genuinely pleased.

That would bode well for their future once he was rid of his current wife.

"I hope your trip went well," Julianna added.

The hallway was empty, but that didn't mean

people weren't listening. He didn't want to be overheard.

"Let's speak in the library where we will not be disturbed." Niko led her past floor-to-ceiling bookcases to a small meeting room.

Julianna ran her fingers along the polished walnut desk. "I had no idea this room was here."

Memories of pestering Stefan while he attempted to study surfaced. Niko pushed the pang of grief aside. "Thank you for offering to help Isabel with her shopping."

"It's the least I can do for you."

Once Stefan had been killed, Niko's life had changed. As the new crown prince, he'd had to put the country's needs above his own. He dated but never seriously. First the war and then lack of time. He'd never had a partner to confide in or ask for help. Perhaps that would change soon. "Thank you."

"You're welcome, but it's not a hardship. I love to shop."

He wasn't about to criticize his current wife to his future spouse, but he didn't want Julianna blindsided. "You may find Isabel a reluctant shopper."

She was a reluctant princess, too.

Julianna didn't appear dissuaded. "I'll convince her a shopping spree is in order."

"I hope you're up for a challenge. Isabel does not want to be a princess."

Julianna smiled knowingly. "Every woman wants

to be a princess even if they would never dare admit the truth aloud."

"Not Isabel." His blood pressure rose thinking about her. "I've never met a woman who tried so hard not to be female."

Julianna furrowed her finely arched brows. "Isabel wants to be a man?"

"No. She is a car mechanic who wears no makeup, dresses, or high heels. She prefers baggy coveralls and casual clothing."

"You sound exasperated."

He sighed. "She is exasperating."

"First impressions can be deceiving," Julianna counseled, making Niko wonder if this was how she spoke to her younger brothers. "Isabel must be in shock to discover her life and past wasn't what she thought."

"The news has stunned her, but my impression isn't far off." Niko thought about her parting words. "Isabel is young. She speaks without thinking. She has no sense of what it is to be royalty."

"She sounds refreshing."

"I thought so yesterday, but today we keep...clashing," he admitted. "She slept so peacefully last night, but when she awoke this morning she was more beast than beauty."

Julianna's mouth quirked. "Isabel is a beauty?"

"Not exactly," he backtracked. "Some men might think she is."

"Do you?"

"She's my wife. I don't think of her in that way."

Amusement gleamed in Julianna's eyes. "I see."

"There's nothing to see," he countered. "Fortunately, Isabel agrees an annulment is the only option. She was excited to hear about you and me getting married."

Julianna sighed.

No doubt relieved the upcoming royal engagement and nuptials could continue as planned.

"We can add her to the wedding party," she said. "A royal wedding can never have too many attendants."

"That is thoughtful of you." And one more reason why Julianna was perfect for his country. "But I doubt Isabel will remain in Vernonia that long."

"You must convince her to stay," Julianna insisted.

"You haven't met her."

"It doesn't matter," Julianna countered. "Isabel has a duty to fulfill here in Vernonia."

"Yes, but Isabel is very"—he searched for a somewhat complimentary adjective—"independent. She has yet to comprehend what fulfilling her duty means."

"All she needs is training. I can help her."

"You don't know what you're offering to take on."

Julianna shook her head. "Come now, you make her sound like an ogre."

"Not an ogre," he admitted. "Ornery."

"I have four younger brothers. I'm used to handling ornery."

"See how shopping goes before you decide if you want to continue helping her or not."

"I can't wait to see what you think of her with a brand-new wardrobe complete with coordinating accessories, shoes, and makeup."

Niko's shoulders tensed. Isabel would never agree to a total makeover. "Just get her into a dress by dinnertime, and I'll be much obliged."

"Obliged enough for another sail tomorrow?" Julianna challenged.

The jaunt to America had wreaked havoc with his schedule. Niko had no free time. But he appreciated Julianna's help because that meant he didn't have to deal with Isabel himself. The woman didn't need a fashion makeover; she needed a complete personality transplant. Niko doubted even the capable Aliestle princess could do much with Isabel by dinnertime. But if Julianna was willing to try...

"If you make her presentable to my parents, I'll find time to sail with you tomorrow."

Lying in bed, Izzy released a long breath—a combination half exhale, half sigh. She didn't want to enjoy being at the castle. She wouldn't fit in no matter what she did. The less attached she got to anyone or anything during her short visit to Vernonia, the better. But right this minute, she couldn't imagine being anywhere else.

Nothing beat floating on a cloud.

Okay, she was lying on a four-poster, queen-size bed, but the mattress was fit for a king. Or a princess. No lumps, bumps, or peas to be found. The feather pillow conformed to the shape of her head, offering the perfect support. The luxurious sheets cocooned her.

Best nap ever.

She never knew a bed could be so comfortable or sheets could feel so soft.

Izzy kept her eyes closed, wanting to linger a little longer. But not too long. She didn't want to throw off her body clock more as Niko had mentioned earlier.

Niko.

As he'd handed her off to the maid, he'd been frowning. Izzy hadn't been as polite as she could have been. Being tired had contributed, but she also didn't appreciate being bossed around. She wasn't one of Niko's subjects. He seemed to forget she was an American. He couldn't tell her what to do.

The image of his ruggedly handsome face formed in her mind. Those to-die-for, blue-green eyes. That dark mane of hair. His killer smile.

Wait. What was she doing thinking about him?

Izzy's eyes sprang open.

Darkness filled the room. That was weird. Natural light had been filtering in through the large windows when she lay down.

Oh, no. Panic spurted through her. Had she slept too long?

Bolting upright, she glanced at the digital clock on the nightstand. Only two-and-a-half hours had passed.

Relief washed over her. But why was the room so dark?

She allowed her vision to adjust.

The yellow damask drapes were closed. They'd been open before she fell asleep.

Uneasy, Izzy squirmed. She lived alone and wasn't used to anyone being around when she slept. A good thing she wouldn't be here long.

She slid from the bed. Her bare feet sank into a thick, colorful rug covering the hardwood floor.

Talk about living large. The grandeur of the interior exceeded the castle's fairy-tale exterior. She felt as if she were staying in a museum with antique furniture, famous paintings, and exquisite tapestries. Afraid she might break a priceless item, she didn't want to touch anything.

Inside the expansive bathroom, Izzy found the plastic gallon-sized bag filled with her toiletries sitting on the gold-veined marble countertop. Someone must have removed it from her duffel bag. She shivered. Having people do everything for her was weird.

A thick, plush, white robe hung on a gold hook.

She ran her fingertips over the soft fabric. The robe was nicer than any of the clothing she'd brought with her. A good thing she was going shopping because nothing she owned would be appropriate to wear at the castle.

Izzy brushed her teeth in the gold sink. Everything was gold, from the faucets to the seals on the fancy soap wrappers. Even the fluffy white towels had gold embroidery on the bottom portion. Uncle Frank would have gotten a kick out of this big bathroom.

She felt a familiar tug at her heart.

Then again, he hadn't been a simple car mechanic. He would have been used to castles with luxurious bathrooms. Living in a motor home had been the opposite extreme.

Had he been hiding her? Or had Uncle Frank wanted to give her as normal a life as possible, not one with gold sinks and her every whim satisfied?

He must have had his reasons.

Good ones.

Aleksander and Evangeline Zvonimir might have been her birth parents, but Frank Miroslav had been Izzy's father. He'd wiped her tears when she hurt herself, boosted her self-confidence when the kids at school teased her for being poor, and taught her everything she knew and loved about cars. He'd saved her life by leaving his family to raise her in another country. She was only beginning to comprehend what he'd given up for her. She couldn't thank him, but Izzy wanted to do something in his honor. Maybe she could tell his relatives how wonderful he'd been to her.

Emotion clogged her throat, but she shook it off. The way she'd learned to do whenever grief appeared unexpected and unwelcome.

A shower would make her feel better, so she turned on the water. As she undressed, steam filled the bathroom, warming the air.

Inside the shower, hot water pulsed down on her as if she were standing in a heated waterfall. She nearly sighed at the decadence of the oversized showerhead.

Comfy beds and amazing bathrooms were perks to being a princess. Izzy hadn't appreciated the invasion of privacy while she slept, but an impressive shower like this could make her forgive and forget most anything.

Normally, she finished showering in minutes because of the RV's tiny water heater and poor water pressure. Not this time. Izzy stayed in until her fingertips shriveled like raisins.

Best shower ever.

She turned off the water, dried off with a towel, slipped into the luxurious robe, and combed her hair.

In the bedroom, she padded to her luggage on the table.

Her backpack was where she'd left it, but her duffel bag was gone. That was odd. The purple would be impossible to miss against the yellow and gold decor.

Maybe whoever placed her toiletries in the

bathroom put away the duffel bag. Izzy checked inside the gilded armoire. Empty hangers hung on the rack. She slid out the two drawers. No bag or clothing. She checked under the bed. Nothing there, either.

This wasn't good. She wanted to get dressed.

Izzy had the clothes she'd worn on the flight, but she didn't want to put on a dirty outfit when she was clean.

Her cell phone was no use. Anyone she could call was half a world away. They couldn't tell her where to find the duffel bag.

She considered the various possibilities. Only one explanation made sense. Someone had taken her bag. To wash the clothes, iron them, burn them—who knew why?

A castle had to have a large staff. She would flag someone down and ask how to contact Mare, the maid who had taken Izzy to the room.

Izzy poked her head out into the hallway. It was empty. Waiting for someone to appear, she shoved her hands into the deep pockets of the robe. No one came.

"Is anyone out there?" she half whispered.

No reply.

Come on. Izzy grew impatient. Maids and butlers should be running around, but no one appeared. That meant she would have to find someone herself. She tightened the belt of her robe.

Stepping into the hallway, Izzy left the door open to remember which room was hers.

The farther she moved away from her room, the more antsy Izzy became. Walking around with wet hair, barefoot, and wearing nothing but a robe wasn't princess-like. A castle probably had rules. Maybe she should return to her room.

Ahead of her, a white-haired man stepped into the hallway. The older gentleman was tall, wore a nice suit, and walked with a slight limp. She noticed he had a prosthetic leg.

No matter what side you were on, we are all marked by the conflict. Some scars are visible. Others are not.

Niko hadn't been kidding. Izzy couldn't believe a man his age had fought in the war. Maybe he'd been a soldier at the beginning. Unless he'd been a casualty. Thinking about what the people of Vernonia had suffered during the civil war hurt her heart.

He headed in the opposite direction.

Oh, no. Izzy couldn't let him get away. "Excuse me."

The man stopped and glanced over his shoulder. His eyes widened.

His reaction told her she must be breaking the dress code. "Do you work here?"

He blinked. "I do."

"Finally."

He studied her with probing green eyes. "Who might you be?"

"I'm Izzy. I arrived this morning from the United States."

"Welcome, Izzy." His smile deepened the lines on his face. "I'm Dee."

"Nice to meet you, Dee." Despite the wrinkles, the man was attractive. "I'm in a bind. My bag with my clothes has disappeared. I searched the room but can't find it."

"Oh, dear, that is a predicament."

She nodded. "I don't imagine trickster ghosts haunt this place?"

"No, though we have our share of skeletons in the closet."

"That's what I figured." She felt more comfortable talking with the staff than royalty. One more reason she wasn't cut out to be a princess. "I'm sure you have work to do, but do you know how I might locate Mare? She was assigned to help me, and I'm wondering if she knows anything about my bag."

"Part of my job is making sure everything runs properly around here."

"Oh, you're the castle manager."

"Something like that." He sounded amused. "I don't know where Mare is, but I know where we can find clothes for you to wear."

"Great."

Dee extended his arm. "Allow me to escort you."

She took his arm. "Thanks."

He walked with a steady stride. His leg didn't slow him down. "What do you think of Vernonia so far, Izzy?"

"I didn't see much during the drive from the airport, but this castle…" She glanced at a fresco painted on the ceiling. "It's straight out of a fairy tale."

"I hope the accommodations are to your liking."

"They're lovely. Thank you. I wanted to stay at a hotel, but Prince Niko wanted me here."

"Are you comfortable?"

"I am. I've had a nice nap and a wonderful shower."

"An excellent start."

Izzy nodded. She wondered if Niko would agree. Earlier he couldn't wait to get away from her. No doubt he wanted her visit to be a short one. She agreed with him on that.

"I believe what you seek is inside here." Dee stopped in front of a pair of wide double doors and opened one. "These ballroom doors are heavier than they look."

She peered inside and gasped. This wasn't a ballroom. This was a clothing store.

Mannequins, decked out in elaborate outfits with matching accessories, fought for space on the parquet floor between racks of clothing and shoes. Stylishly dressed women bustled about in short skirts and high heels, carrying purses, lingerie, and shoes. A mix of perfumes lingered in the air.

The room was a pumped-up, steroid-version of *What Not to Wear*. This was so not the shopping Izzy had in mind. She struggled to breathe.

Some might tingle with excitement at the thought of being let loose among the clothes and shoes, but the sight filled Izzy with dread. Fashion didn't interest her. She was into comfort, not style. Worse, these women had gone to all this trouble for her. Niko and Jovan, too.

Near a three-paneled mirror, a man stood, out of place among the feminine finery.

Not just a man. Niko.

He'd showered, shaved, and changed suits. Handsome. A few of the other women who kept stealing glances his way must think so, too.

Niko didn't seem to notice. He was engaged in a conversation with a gorgeous blond supermodel. Feeling more out of place than before, Izzy crossed her arms over her chest.

Dee cleared his throat.

Conversations stopped. Women froze in place. Heads bowed. Gazes lowered. Everyone grew still except for Niko, who hurried across the room toward Izzy.

She moved closer to Dee. "What's happening?"

"Do not worry. Everything is fine, Izzy."

Niko stared intently at her, making her question the "fine" part.

His brows furrowed. "What are you—"

"Izzy's bag with her clothing disappeared from her room," Dee said, rather bravely Izzy thought, considering the fierce expression on Niko's face. "I offered her my assistance."

"The women needed her sizes, so they borrowed her bag, Father."

Realization hit Izzy. She inhaled sharply. "Dee as in Dmitar."

"Yes, my dear," Dee said.

"Oh, no." Cheeks burning, she pulled the robe tighter as if she could somehow disappear into its folds. "You're the king, the one who emailed me about the box, and I'm an idiot."

"Father—"

King Dmitar held up his hand the way Niko had done with Jovan.

Niko remained silent. Izzy had forgotten about that trick, but she made a mental note to remember it for later.

"You're not an idiot, Izzy," King Dmitar said kindly. "You are delightful. I see the best of your parents in you."

Emotion tightened her throat. "Thank you, Your Majesty."

"As for my son..." King Dmitar turned his attention to Niko. "Izzy does not know our ways. She should not be left on her own and forced to figure out where her clothing disappeared to."

Niko bowed his head. "Yes, sir."

King Dmitar focused on her. "And a suggestion, Izzy."

"Yes, Dee." She cringed at her lapse. "I mean,

Your Majesty."

"Queen Beatrice dislikes the color pink. You may wish to keep that in mind while shopping."

"Thanks for the tip, sir." Izzy smiled. "I'm not much into pink myself."

"Excellent." The king eyed the racks of dresses. "The queen likes the color purple. As do I."

"I'll remember that, sir. Thank you."

He focused on each person in the room until his gaze rested on the stunning blonde who had been talking with Niko. The king pressed his lips together. "I see you are in good hands. I will leave you to your shopping."

With that, he left.

As soon as the door closed, the women returned to carrying accessories to the mannequins. The blonde who had been speaking with Niko supervised them.

Izzy blew out a puff of air. "I can't believe that was your father."

Niko stood next to her with an irritated expression. "Who did you think he was?"

"The castle manager."

Niko laughed. "I suppose that is one of his job responsibilities."

"You're not helping."

He raised a brow. "I didn't think you needed anyone's help."

Izzy made a face.

"You may have trouble finding an outfit to

coordinate with your expression," he teased.

"I'm sure I can find an outfit to match every expression and one to wear each hour of the day. I thought I was going shopping at a store or a mall." She motioned to the clothing. "It's a bit much, don't you think?"

"Not for a princess. There will be dinners, outings, appearances at the High Court."

"I won't be here that long."

"Long enough."

Izzy tried to take it all in. Tried and failed. "I'm beginning to understand what Cinderella might have felt like."

"Except in your case, the shoe already fits."

"But we want to get it off as soon as possible."

"That is the plan." He sounded excited.

Izzy set her chin. "You know, dude. I want the annulment as badly as you do, but you don't have to be rude about it."

Before he could reply, the supermodel hurried over on high heels as if she were wearing tennis shoes. She probably taught Pilates, cooked like a gourmet chef, and rescued orphans from third-world countries in her spare time. The woman's smile showed off two rows of perfectly spaced, white teeth. The boys at the garage would be comatose in her presence. "You must be Princess Isabel."

"Isabel," Niko said. "This is Her Royal Highness Princess Julianna Von Schneckel of Aliestle."

Julianna. Niko's girlfriend and future wife. She was also a princess. No wonder he couldn't wait to annul the marriage and marry a woman who exuded so much confidence and beauty a *Sports Illustrated* swimsuit model would be intimidated.

Izzy was out of her element in every possible way. She forced her foot to stop tapping.

Julianna extended her arm. Everything about the princess was perfect, right down to her manicured and polished fingernails. "It's wonderful to meet you, Isabel."

She shook her hand. Julianna's grip was firm and her hands rougher than Izzy expected them to be. "And you."

Niko watched them. No doubt comparing his current wife to his future one.

A chilling thought inched its way along Izzy's spine. She hoped he wasn't planning to stay while she tried on clothing. This experience would be difficult enough without him here watching or, worse, providing commentary.

"Thanks for arranging all this, Niko." Izzy tried to sound as cheerful as she could. "I'm sure you have better things to do with your time so don't feel obligated to stick around. As your father said, I'm in good hands."

"You're in excellent hands," Niko said. "But I have a few minutes before my meeting."

Bummer.

"You keep Isabel company, Niko," Julianna said. "I want to get everyone in their places."

People had places? Izzy took a deep breath and exhaled slowly.

"It won't be that bad," Niko said, as soon as Julianna was out of earshot.

"Want to trade places?" Izzy asked.

"My legs aren't meant for dresses."

"Mine, either. I mean, I haven't worn a dress since..." Uncle Frank's funeral. "It's been a while."

"You'll look fine."

She shrugged. "New clothing won't make me a princess."

"Whether you wear a pair of coveralls or a Chanel dress, you are a princess." He sounded annoyed. "But new clothing might help you feel more comfortable here."

She gazed at the large crystal chandeliers hanging from the ballroom ceiling. "I don't think that's possible."

"You only just arrived."

Izzy watched Julianna. "I'm not like her."

"Her?"

"Your girlfriend. Princess Julianna."

"I never thought you were like her." Niko spoke in a matter-of-fact tone. "You said you needed clothing, so I arranged for you to go shopping."

"I should learn to keep my mouth shut."

"Perhaps." He sounded amused. "But this is a gift,

Isabel. I appreciate you coming all this way to settle matters. Please indulge yourself. Even if you never plan on wearing the clothing once you leave, you can donate them to a worthy cause."

That was some gift. Royalty were different than normal folk. "You're wasting money doing this."

"The expense is irrelevant."

"Maybe for you." She forced herself to stand tall. "But for me, this would buy a lot of race car."

A knowing smile played at the corner of his mouth. "Noted."

Something connected them. Izzy didn't know what, but she couldn't look away. Truth was, she didn't want to.

"Have you two finished sparring so we can shop?" Julianna asked playfully.

As Niko's gaze left Izzy's, an odd sense of rejection settled over her. It must be jet lag.

He focused on his future bride. "Yes."

"Then off with you." Julianna motioned toward the doors. "Your presence will make Isabel uncomfortable."

He nodded once. "Enjoy the shopping, ladies."

Izzy watched him leave. "You need to teach me how to do that."

"I will teach you many things. How to handle a prince is only one of them."

She shook her head. "I don't think I could handle Niko like that."

"I believe you already have." Julianna smiled mischievously. "Ready to shop till you drop?"

"Not really." Izzy wondered what the princess had meant by her first sentence. Then again, maybe Izzy was reading too much into things. "I'm not big on shopping and clothes. I've always been a tomboy. Cars interest me more than makeup, hair, and shoes."

Julianna's grin widened. "Then it's good you have me."

Chapter Nine

That evening, Niko stood in the dining room with Julianna, waiting for his parents and Isabel to arrive. Servants scurried about like mice. Instead of carrying crumbs and cheese, they held pitchers of water and platters.

Anticipation filled the air. Niko felt himself caught up in the excitement. Everyone wanted a glimpse of Princess Isabel. Unfortunately, she was far from the princess they were expecting. She might be here by birthright, but she believed a wrench belonged in her hand, not a scepter. He wanted her to see otherwise.

He checked his watch. "Isabel is late."

"Isabel is not late." Julianna swirled her champagne flute.

She wore a lovely green cocktail dress and silver heels. He recognized the diamond earrings and necklace from the Aliestle crown jewel collection. He couldn't picture Isabel in a similar outfit, but whatever she wore tonight had to be an improvement over her regular attire.

"A princess needs to make an entrance." Julianna stared over the lip of her glass. "Anxious to see Isabel?"

"Anxious to know how much damage control I must do. Perhaps she has decided not to attend."

"Oh, believe me, she'll be here." Julianna's tone suggested she knew a secret. "By the way, the wind should be perfect for a sail tomorrow."

"We shall see."

"The wind? Or your wife?"

"Both." Niko liked Julianna. No chemistry existed between them, but a friendship was growing. That would be a good foundation for a marriage. Perhaps, in time, passion would enter the relationship. Then again, he'd heard passion was fleeting, so perhaps friendship would be enough. "Though the latter will soon be..."

Footsteps sounded outside the dining room.

A woman wearing a lavender dress stood in the wide doorway with a hesitant expression on her gorgeous face.

His heart rate kicked up a notch.

What a beauty. Her brown hair was piled on the top of her head, secured by an invisible clip of some sort. Soft tendrils framed her oval face. But her expressive eyes... They mesmerized him.

"So what time should we leave on our sail tomorrow?" Julianna sounded amused.

"Time?" He couldn't stop staring at the vision in the doorway.

Julianna laughed. "The makeover definitely worked."

Niko did a double take. "Isabel?"

"She cleans up well, don't you think?"

He'd seen her cleaned up but not like this. All he could do was stare captivated. Isabel was...stunning.

"I can't believe you said she reminds you of a man," Julianna continued quietly. "She may not like the color pink and prefer motor oil to moisturizer, but she's quite feminine."

"I see that."

The above-the-knee hem of her dress showed off Isabel's long legs. He hoped she would wear more shorter dresses. Legs like hers needed to be shown off, not hidden beneath coveralls, jeans, and bathrobes.

"Though I will admit, the rest of her princess transformation may take more time," Julianna said. "Isabel says whatever is on her mind. She has no filter. That must stop or the media will take advantage of her."

"I have no doubt in your abilities."

"I had fun. Izzy may not be a typical princess, but she's a charming young woman."

"Izzy?"

"That's what her friends call her."

Isabel had mentioned being called Izzy, but he preferred her full name, enjoyed the way the syllables rolled off his tongue. Izzy sounded too...pedestrian. But there was nothing dull or unimaginative about her now. The lavender complemented her pale complexion. The style flattered her figure. She looked like a princess. "I doubt her friends would recognize her."

"*You* didn't."

"Shock."

"Nothing more?" Julianna asked.

Attraction, desire, lust. But he knew better than to mention those things to his future wife. "Nothing else."

"Be a dear, Niko, and escort her into the dining room." Julianna sounded genuinely pleased with his reaction. "Izzy's still trying to master the art of walking in high heels. I'd hate to see her make a mistake and berate herself over it."

He didn't have to be asked twice. He glanced at Julianna, who appeared almost smug with satisfaction. "I shall return with your work of art."

As he approached Isabel, Niko was even more impressed by her transformation. The expert makeup application complemented her high cheekbones. Her glossed lips sparkled. Flecks of gold danced in her irises. Julianna had outdone herself. "You are lovely, Isabel."

"Thanks."

Niko caught a whiff of her vanilla and jasmine scent. That hadn't changed, and he was glad.

"I feel like a fraud," Isabel whispered.

He didn't understand the agitation in her voice. She should be pleased with the makeover. "Why a fraud?"

"I'm still me. Only the outer packaging has changed," she explained. "With all this makeup on, I must look like a clown. I'm sure in this dress and high heels, I could be mistaken for a street corner hooker."

Niko winced. "No one would mistake you for anything but a princess."

Too bad she didn't act or speak like one.

"I appreciate that," she said. "Even if it's not one hundred percent true."

He extended his arm. "May I?"

"Royalty is big on escorting."

"It is part of our prince training."

"Is princess training available?" she asked.

"Yours has already started."

She pursed her glossed lips. "I was kidding."

He raised a brow. "I am not."

She eyed his arm warily before placing her hand over his.

A jolt of awareness startled Niko. Perhaps static

electricity explained the shock.

"Just so you know," she whispered. "I'm only allowing you to escort me so I don't end up spread-eagled on the floor with my new lace thong showing."

Niko's gaze drifted lower.

What was he doing?

Abruptly, he focused on her face. Anywhere else was unacceptable. He would have preferred not knowing what type of lingerie she wore underneath her dress. The image plastered across his brain would take time to erase. "I will make sure that doesn't happen."

For both their sakes.

Isabel took a tentative step, teetering on her heels. "I don't know why anyone would strap these torture devices to their feet."

"Why did you?"

"Princess Julianna told me I had to. A closet full of shoes seems to be a prerequisite for being a princess. But none are allowed to be comfortable."

The exasperation in her voice made him smile. He led her into the dining room with nary a stumble.

Her lips parted. "Wow."

Niko understood her awe. The room was the definition of impressive with its marble fireplace, gold damask-covered walls, chandeliers, and the long, rectangular table set with fine china, sparkling crystal, freshly cut flowers, and a candelabra full of lit candles.

"No wonder you dress for dinner around here," she added. "Black tie not optional."

Julianna joined them. "Good evening, Izzy."

"Hey, Jules."

The familiarity between the two women surprised Niko. Shopping must quicken the bonds of feminine friendship. Perhaps Jovan had been correct about Julianna becoming Isabel's role model.

A waiter appeared with the tray of champagne flutes. Niko took one and handed the glass to Isabel.

"No, thanks." She waved him off. "Tonight will be difficult enough without adding alcohol to the mix. I doubt your parents would appreciate me dancing on the table."

No, but Niko wouldn't mind too much. He did, however, approve of her good judgment in refusing to drink.

Isabel studied a place setting. "I might have better luck dancing than trying to figure out what silverware and glass to use when."

"Go from the outside in." He remembered the etiquette lessons forced on him even during wartime.

"Watch what we do," Julianna added. "You'll be fine."

Two little lines appeared above Isabel's nose. She rubbed her hands together as if nervous. "Maybe I should get a plate to go."

A flurry of noise sounded in the doorway. Niko stiffened. "My parents have arrived."

"Don't worry." Julianna touched Isabel's shoulder. "Just remember what I told you earlier."

Isabel nodded, but she bit her lower lip. Uncertainty filled her eyes.

The urge to reach out to her was strong, but Niko was uncertain what to do given Julianna's presence. Protocol instruction hadn't covered this situation.

His father entered the dining room with a rare smile. "What a lovely dress, Izzy."

Niko appreciated the way his father used her nickname. The king could intimidate the most seasoned statesman, but he seemed to be trying to put Isabel at ease.

She curtsied. "Thank you, sir."

"May I introduce you to my wife, Her Royal Majesty Queen Beatrice." His father presented Niko's mother, who wore a floor-length ball gown, a diamond necklace, and matching tiara. No one would mistake her for anything but the queen. "Beatrice, this is Isabel, but her friends call her Izzy."

Niko nearly rolled his eyes. His mother would never call Isabel by anything other than her given name.

"We are delighted to have you in Vernonia, Izzy." His mother's eyes twinkled like the jewels around her neck. "You've been away far too long."

What? Niko stared in disbelief.

"It's a pleasure to meet you, Your Royal Majesty." Isabel curtsied again, only this time she swayed on her heels like a tree in a windstorm. A soft gasp escaped her lips. Panic flashed on her face.

Niko grabbed her elbow so she wouldn't tip over.

She mouthed a thank you before shrugging off his hand. She didn't appear any steadier on her feet so he kept hold of her. "Isabel is recovering from the long flight. I'm sure she would like to sit down."

"Of course." His father motioned everyone to the table. "We have much to discuss."

"Yes, we do." His mother sat, and a waiter handed her a napkin. "But now that I've seen Izzy myself, I agree with you, Dee. We won't have any trouble."

Sitting across the table from him, Isabel's forehead wrinkled.

"Trouble, Mother?" Niko asked, curious what she meant.

"Your father and I have been discussing Izzy's future," she said.

That set off an alarm in Niko's head. Waiters brought out the first course and set the bowls of soup on the table at the same time.

"That's nice of you all." Izzy's smile appeared forced. "But it's unnecessary, Your Highnesses."

"But it is necessary," his father countered. "All this must be a shock to you, Izzy, but we are your family now. We don't have much time. We must plan for what happens next."

"An annulment comes next." Niko didn't want his parents getting involved when everything was set. "We will go to the High Court first thing Monday morning."

Izzy nodded. "You don't need to waste your time

planning anything, sir. My future is set."

"I appreciate your concern over my time." His father's expression was earnest. "But I believe you need a history lesson."

Niko took a sip of his chilled eggplant soup. His father's lessons usually lasted until the wee hours of the morning.

"You, Izzy, are the last of the royal Sachestian bloodline that ruled the northern region before joining with the southern portion of the country to form Vernonia," his father continued. "For centuries, the Separatists asked that your bloodline rule the north again. But the Loyalists wanted the Kresimir bloodline to rule over all the land. The two groups hotly disagreed and fights would break out."

"A little like the Montagues and the Capulets?" Izzy asked.

Niko nearly laughed. "No star-crossed lovers, however."

"But still Shakespearean," his mother added.

Julianna nodded. "History has shown a marriage between rival sides can ease strife and lead to peace."

"Excellent point, Julianna." His father took a sip of water. "Over time, the arguments between the Separatists and the Loyalists intensified, Izzy. An official petition to separate the northern portion of Vernonia circulated. Civil war seemed imminent. Your father believed a union between the two royal families would appease the Separatists and avoid war. His goal, our goal, was to unite Vernonia with your marriage. But the civil unrest became violent with terrorist acts. The people remained divided, and war broke out."

Silence enveloped the room.

Isabel toyed with her napkin. She hadn't tasted the soup yet. "It must have been a horrible time, Your Majesty."

"Horrible does not begin to describe the war, my dear. Our country has been at peace for five years." His father hesitated. "But that didn't happen until after the last of the royal Sachestian bloodline was killed during the conflict. The Separatists believed, they still believe, no Sachestian descendants remain. But now you have returned like a Phoenix from the ashes—"

"Let's not tell them I'm here. No one has to know about me," Izzy interrupted. "I'm sorry for butting in, sir, but your country has been through enough turmoil. I'm not here to cause any problems. The truth is, I don't want to be a princess. Let's get the marriage annulled. If you're unable to transfer my father's estate, we'll figure something else out so I can disappear from Vernonia forever."

"That sounds like an excellent plan." Niko was proud of her for speaking up and succinctly saying what needed to be said. That was one positive to Isabel's lack of princess skills. Julianna would have remained quiet.

"I wish it were that simple." Regret filled his father's voice. "We cannot pretend the Separatists do not exist."

"Julianna's father supported the Separatists during the war," Niko countered. "They support my marriage to her."

"Yes, but they do not know about Isabel."

"Father—"

"Imagine you are a Separatist." His father's expression grew more serious. "You have agreed per the peace accord to be a part of a new united Vernonia. You believe the members of your royal family are dead but suddenly discover one young princess lives. Oh, the joy. Until you learn the crown prince of your country has annulled his marriage to your princess, so he can wed a different princess from another country. How do you think that will go over in this so-called united land?"

"You make it sound as if I'm being slighted, sir." Isabel's gaze never wavered from the king's. "I want the annulment. I don't want to be married to Niko."

Her firm tone left no doubt she wanted out of the marriage as much as Niko did. She'd mentioned that before, but the rejection stung. "Our marriage was only to avoid a civil war, Father. The war is over. The custom that allowed us to wed is now illegal. An annulment makes sense."

"Perception can be as strong a motivator as reality," his father lectured. "Vernonians have quick tempers. Our loyalty is our strength but also our biggest weakness. We will cling to our causes until the bitter end. Whether right or wrong."

Niko stiffened in shock. "I hope you are not suggesting we remain married, sir."

Isabel's mouth formed another perfect O. She appeared aghast at the idea.

Julianna leaned forward with interest. Niko couldn't believe she was sitting here with their engagement on the line without speaking up.

His father's gaze sharpened. "You have made it clear that is not an option."

Isabel's shoulders dropped. Her features relaxed.

Julianna leaned against her chair, but her lips were pressed together. Her expression was unreadable.

Niko would have expected her to be happier. Perhaps she was nervous about his father's intentions. Niko would put her at ease. "Marrying Julianna is best for Vernonia. No offense, Isabel."

"None taken," she said without hesitation.

"So you've mentioned over and over again." His father looked at Julianna and then Isabel. "That leaves me no choice but to find Isabel another husband. One she must marry the minute the annulment is granted."

"What?" Isabel shrieked.

"Why?" Julianna asked, sounding taken aback.

"Father." Niko had brought Isabel to Vernonia. He didn't want her to be forced into an arranged marriage. "You can't be serious."

"I am," his father said. "If Izzy is married, the Separatists can be upset, but they won't be able to change the situation. If she remains single..."

Dread pulsed through Niko's veins. "They could demand we remarry or use her to rally against you."

"Yes," his father agreed.

Niko thought he'd considered every angle. He believed the Separatists were content with their coalition in the government and comfortable with his family as heads of state. He was so focused on modernizing that he never thought they would demand a marriage alliance in the face of improved economic development. But apparently he had been wrong. Because of that, Isabel would be the one to pay. She did not deserve to have her life plans derailed more than they had been.

"No." Isabel's face paled. "There has to be another way. Anything..."

He respected the way she stood up for herself. "Please give us time to think of an alternative, Father."

"The High Court convenes on Monday," his father said. "You have one day to come up with a plan that will maintain peace. Otherwise Izzy must get married."

"Who do you plan to marry her off to?" Niko couldn't think of anyone in the kingdom that would be a match. The thought of her with another man...

Stop. He needed to reel in his thoughts.

"I've been working on that, dear." His mother watched Izzy with interest. "I have a list of eligible royals I've come up with..."

THE RELUCTANT PRINCESS

Chapter Ten

Talk about a living nightmare. Izzy needed to find a way to keep from being married off to a name on the queen's list. And fast. Her future—her happiness—was at stake.

As she lay in bed, her mind raced fast enough to capture the pole position at Darlington Raceway. The clock read 2:04. No way she could sleep. Not with the conversation at dinner replaying in her mind like reruns of a TV show.

This situation could be its own series, a reality TV show called *The Royal Kresimirs*. The preview would consist of shots of each of them. King Dmitar saying Izzy needed to marry. Queen Beatrice rattling off names of potential husbands. Prince Niko interjecting his opinion on each man. Princess Julianna smiling as she attempted to keep the peace. Izzy racking her brain to find a way out of being forced to marry a stranger.

But this was too far-fetched to be a television show. Nothing like this should happen. Not in the twenty-first century. Not to an American citizen.

That gave Izzy an idea.

She could call the Embassy. Surely the State Department would help her out.

No, that would only solve her problem, not...Vernonia's.

Izzy wasn't attached to this strange country. Until yesterday, she'd only heard of the place in the news, but Vernonia had been important to her parents and to Uncle Frank. She wasn't selfish enough to ignore the war fought here or pretend another couldn't happen.

Her stomach growled.

She'd been so upset she couldn't eat dinner. She'd turned down the chocolate torte served for dessert. That had been dumb. Chocolate always lifted her spirits. She might be able to find leftovers in the kitchen.

She crawled out of bed, shrugged on the white bathrobe over her pajamas, and stepped into the hallway. Still unsure if she would recognize which room was hers, she left the door open like she had earlier.

Three wrong turns later, Izzy sat in the castle's deserted kitchen, poking at a slice of chocolate torte with her fork. Her appetite remained missing despite her tummy's grumblings. She couldn't muster enough enthusiasm to take a bite of chocolate.

Pathetic.

"Here you are." Niko's voice cut through the silence, startling her. "I wondered where you had disappeared to."

"How did you know I was gone?"

"The door to your room was open." He went past the wall of stainless steel refrigerators and around the massive commercial stoves.

"All the doors look alike."

He was wearing the same dress shirt and pants as earlier, but he'd ditched the jacket and tie. He'd also unbuttoned the collar and rolled up the sleeves. The casual style made Niko seem approachable, more like a normal guy than a crown prince.

"I left mine open so I wouldn't go into the wrong room," she added.

"Smart move. I called your name, but you didn't answer." He sat in the chair next to her. "I thought you might have run away."

"The first thing I thought of doing was running away." Izzy stared at the uneaten torte. "But I crossed it off the list."

"You have a list?"

"Well, yeah." She stabbed the fork into the torte.

"This doesn't affect you, but we're talking about my future. I won't grab a splash of gas and hope I can finish the race. I need a full tank before I approach your father."

"What happens to you affects me, Isabel." Niko's lips thinned. "Why do you think *I'm* awake?"

"Don't worry. I'll come up with something." Izzy had no choice because the alternative... She shivered. "Enjoy your time with Julianna. You could be with her right now."

"I'm sure she's asleep, and you shouldn't be alone." His jaw tightened. "I've been trying to figure out a solution. If I had known this would happen, I would have never brought you to Vernonia."

"You didn't know."

"But I should have." His expression appeared contrite. "We need to find a way out of this."

We. Izzy didn't feel so alone. She didn't like needing help, but she wasn't getting very far on her own.

He eyed her torte suspiciously. "Are you going to eat that?"

"No."

"May I?"

She pushed the plate toward him. "It's all yours."

"Thank you." He raised the fork. "What stopped you from running away?"

"Logistics," she admitted. "I can't return home without a passport or cash."

"Ah, yes. You only have the temporary Vernonian passport Jovan arranged for you."

Izzy nodded. "But Jovan has it."

"If you want the passport—"

"If I ran away, you wouldn't be able to get an annulment. That means you couldn't marry Jules without committing bigamy." Izzy also feared his parents might send someone to bring her back unless she went into hiding. She didn't want to do that.

"Thank you for sticking around. I'm much obliged, as will Julianna be." He scooped up a forkful of torte. "I thought of one possibility. It's extreme, however."

"I'm open to anything, including extreme."

He raised the fork. "How about faking your death?"

"That's on my list."

The edges of his mouth curved. "Great minds think alike."

"It's a good idea." Izzy had been mulling over that one. "I don't want to die, but if people thought I was dead, any issues with the Separatists would die, too. No one would complain if you married Julianna."

"The logistics would be more complicated than running away."

She nodded. "There can't be a body."

"That limits how a person can die."

"There has to be a way to fake a death."

"Fire," Niko suggested.

"Wouldn't bones and teeth remain?" she asked.

"Yes, unless an inferno killed you, but a fire might be dangerous to pull off."

"I wouldn't want anyone to get hurt."

"Of course not." He rubbed his chin. That sexy razor stubble had reappeared. "You could drown."

"Bodies disappear at sea never to be seen again."

Niko nodded. "Julianna is a world-class sailor. You could fall overboard."

"I like the drowning part, but do you want to involve your future wife? It's probably illegal."

"No, she should not be involved."

That meant it was only the two of them. Partners in crime. "I could fall into the sea. Off a boat or a cliff."

"You will have to say goodbye to Isabel Poussard forever."

"You're right." She tried to imagine what it would be like. "I wouldn't be six-foot-under dead, but everyone who knows me would have to think I died."

"There would be no going back."

No going back.

She could never do anything racing-related. But she would lose more than that dream. She pictured her friends in Charlotte—Rowdy, Boyd, and the rest of the guys at the garage.

Her chest tightened.

If she married a royal, her life would be different, but she could visit her friends. Faking her death would mean never talking to them again. She would be on her own. No past to speak about. No one to turn to if she needed a friend or...anything.

"Honestly, I don't think I could let my friends believe I was dead..." She shook her head. "Not after the hurt and grief we suffered through when Uncle Frank died."

"I would rather not have to lie or break any laws, either."

She slumped in the chair. "We're back where we started."

"We will think of a solution."

Niko sounded confident, but a strange sensation settled in the pit of her stomach, one having nothing to do with not eating dinner. She had no way out of this mess. The reality of the situation seemed...undeniable. "I'm not sure there is another way."

He set his fork on the plate. "Isabel—"

"Think about it." She fought a rising panic. "We're both awake in the middle of the night, trying to figure this out. Faking my death is the best idea we came up with."

"We just need time."

"It's Sunday." A lump formed in her throat. "We don't have much longer."

"That means..."

Tears stung. "I know what it means."

"You don't want to get married to someone else."

"No." She blew out a frustrated breath. "But when I think what might happen if I don't..."

This wasn't a debate about differences between

two political parties and their views on issues. People were willing to kill for what they wanted. Her parents had been murdered, and her uncle Frank had given up his way of life in Vernonia because of the conflict between the Separatists and the Loyalists. Izzy had wanted to honor her family. Maybe getting married was a way to do that.

She blinked to keep the tears at bay. "I don't think I have any choice."

Niko covered Izzy's hand with his. She relished the touch of comfort, but it was also a harsh reminder that another man, a stranger, would soon be her husband. He would be the one touching her.

She'd never had a serious boyfriend. She could count on one hand the number of men she'd kissed. She'd never done anything more than that, but once she was married...

Hot tears spilled down her cheeks.

She angled away so Niko wouldn't see her cry.

He cupped her chin and turned her face toward him. Gently he wiped the tears from her cheeks with his fingers. "I will not allow you to be forced into a marriage you do not want."

"Thanks, but this is bigger than you and me. People have suffered so much already. My parents and Uncle Frank sacrificed their lives. I won't be the catalyst for more violence and pain."

"I did not believe you had what it takes to be a princess, but I was wrong. You do. You have an innate sense of royal duty," Niko said. "My apologies for misjudging you, Isabel."

The sincerity in his voice brought another round of tears. She would miss hearing him say her name.

"Thanks." Izzy sniffled. "I'm usually not so girly about things."

"It's okay." Niko gathered her into his arms.

Izzy stiffened. She didn't need him to hold her, but she had no desire to leave his embrace. Loneliness made her relax and lean toward him so he could pull her closer.

Pressing against his hard chest, the beat of his heart—steady and strong—sounded against her cheek. Invisible warmth enveloped her.

For the first time since Uncle Frank's death, she felt safe. Accepted. The emotions she'd been holding in for so long poured out. She couldn't stop the tears from falling.

Niko didn't soothe her with platitudes. He held her, rubbing her back. It was more than she had expected from him but was all she needed.

She didn't know how long Niko kept his arms around her. Slowly her breathing settled. Her tears stopped. Somehow, in his arms, Izzy found the strength she needed to accept her fate.

"I know what I have to do. It's just..." She took a breath and another. "I can't imagine having to spend the rest of my life married to a man who was forced to be my husband. It seems so wrong."

He brushed his hand through her hair. "You are not used to the concept. But arranged marriages are not all bad. There's friendship, companionship, and having a common purpose. Not to mention, children."

His closeness comforted her. Izzy could almost believe things would be better than the nightmare in her head. "I only wish..."

"Tell me."

Izzy hesitated, but Niko had been so caring, so kind she had to tell him. "I wish instead of marrying some random royal with a fancy title I could marry for love. But at this point, I'd settle for being able to choose who I married."

Niko continued to comb his fingers through her hair. "Whom would you choose?"

He popped into her mind. Stupid. The emotion of the situation, his compassion, was making her feel closer to him.

"Tell me who," he pressed.

None of her dates had liked cars or racing the way she did. The guy she spent the most time with was Boyd. Building go-carts, working at dirt tracks on pit crews, watching races. They shared the same interests and the same dream but weren't...romantic. Still, that would be better than the alternative.

When she thought of it like that, the decision was easy to make. "Boyd."

"Your coworker?" Niko stiffened. "You said he wasn't your boyfriend."

"He's not, but he's my closest friend. He wouldn't expect us to have, um, a real marriage."

"You mean sex."

Her cheeks burned. "Yes."

"You would be satisfied with a marriage in name only?"

"It isn't about being, um, satisfied." She shouldn't have mentioned this. "We wouldn't have to be married for decades. Only a few years. Long enough for the political unrest to stabilize in Vernonia and for you and Jules to have kids. Then Boyd and I could divorce."

A gasp—or something similar to that—sounded.

Izzy peered over Niko's shoulder. "What was that noise?"

"I didn't hear anything."

She glanced in that direction again but saw no one. Must have been one of the refrigerators. "Do you think your father would allow me to marry Boyd?"

"We can ask him. Would Boyd marry you?"

"Probably. People have assumed we're a couple for years. We know each other well." She pictured her coworker and friend. Boyd was an all-American, beef-fed Southerner. Down home and down-to-earth. Strong and rugged, but kindhearted like Niko. Not model handsome, but many women found Boyd attractive. "I think he'd say yes because of our friendship, but if I told him I wanted to start a race team together, that would seal the deal. He's more car crazy than I am."

Niko's mouth twisted. "Would you be happy married to Boyd?"

"Marriage has never been on my radar screen, but..."

She thought about her parents and Uncle Frank. Marrying a man she loved like a brother was nothing compared to the sacrifices they had made. She would do this for them.

"If Vernonia remains at peace, then yes. I would be happy married to Boyd."

Niko let go of her. "We shall take this alternative to my father in the morning."

"That's only a few hours away." Izzy felt cold without his arms around her. "Fingers crossed he says yes."

"Vernonia is indebted to you, Isabel." The way Niko spoke made her heart bump. "And so am I."

She didn't care about Vernonia, but him... His face was so close to hers. Something—passion, perhaps—flashed in his eyes and heated her blood. He tilted his head.

Was Niko going to kiss her?

Izzy's pulse rate skyrocketed. Her mouth went dry.

Heaven help her, she wanted to kiss him.

She parted her lips in anticipation.

Niko raised her hand to his mouth and kissed the top. The brush of his lips was soft, a caress.

She nearly sighed.

He lowered her hand. "If there is anything you

need..."

She needed him to kiss her. Not her hand, but her lips.

Here. Now.

Niko released her hand.

Disappointment shot through her. No matter how much she wanted this moment to mean something more than one person comforting another, it didn't.

It couldn't.

Izzy might want her lips to be crushed by his, but Niko was too honorable. He would never hold her passionately. He would never share his dreams with her. He would never whisper endearments into her ear.

Those were things he would do with...Jules.

Niko would marry the pretty, perfect princess from Aliestle. And if the king said yes, Izzy would marry Boyd. When she arrived in the United States, she would have a husband with her. They would join the world of racing, not as members of a pit crew, but as the owners of a new racing team.

Izzy would have everything she wanted. And so would Niko.

A happy ending for everyone involved, including Vernonia.

There was only one problem.

Why didn't she feel happier?

Chapter Eleven

The next morning, Niko sat next to Isabel on a settee in the king's private drawing room. His father, wearing his typical suit and tie, stood across from them. A stern expression was on his face as he considered their request.

The silence increased Niko's discomfort level. He would rather be elsewhere, but he didn't want Isabel to go through this alone. She deserved his support for what she was willing to do for him and Vernonia.

Isabel rested her clasped hands on her lap. She wore a teal skirt and matching jacket. The heels on her shoes weren't as high as last night, making it easier for her to walk. She looked like a princess in the outfit.

The dark circles beneath her eyes belied her appearance. Those, however, were the only clue anything was wrong. He'd still place his money on her. The defiant tilt of her chin told him she was ready to fight.

His father had no idea whom he was dealing with. As Niko had learned last night, neither did he. Isabel was a strong woman. Beautiful and so much more than he imagined she would be.

Thinking of her had kept Niko awake the rest of the night. Each time he'd closed his eyes, his senses came alive, remembering the scent of her hair, the taste of her skin, and the warmth in her heart. He never imagined having those feelings for her. Physical attraction explained part of his reaction, but the biggest reason for his respect and admiration was her willingness to do what benefited Vernonia. That combined into a potent mix of...affection.

A warning alarm blared in his head.

These were feelings he should have about Julianna, not Isabel. Niko was anxious to get this matter resolved. He couldn't allow unwanted and unwarranted emotions for the American to cloud his thoughts.

His father paced. "There is much to consider here."

Isabel's lower lip trembled. Only slightly, but her vulnerability pressed against Niko like a two-ton weight. She'd been uncomfortable crying in front of him. She wanted to handle her own affairs, but he couldn't sit and do nothing while she was upset.

He covered her hand with his and squeezed.

The edges of her mouth lifted in a closed-mouth smile.

His heart beating faster, he smiled back.

The lines on his father's forehead deepened.

As Niko's shoulder muscles tensed, he realized his father was staring at Niko's hand on top of Isabel's.

Niko pulled his arm away. Not that he should feel guilty. Holding hands wasn't the same as kissing her. He may have thought about kissing her last night, but today he'd merely offered a gesture of comfort. The fact he enjoyed holding her hand was of no consequence.

Gratitude. That described his feelings toward Isabel. Appreciation for the sacrifice she was willing to make, too. Nothing...more.

"You are satisfied with this alternative, Izzy?" his father asked finally.

"Satisfied is a relative term, Father," Niko answered. "This marriage is being forced upon Isabel."

His father glared at him. "Your name is not Izzy."

Niko pressed his lips together.

"I'd rather not have to marry at all, sir," Isabel answered honestly with her head held high. "But I will be more satisfied with this option than what was proposed at dinner."

His father rubbed his chin. He usually made decisions quickly, but this was taking longer than it should.

That worried Niko. Isabel hadn't eaten breakfast. Her tiredness suggested she hadn't slept. She needed the situation to be resolved.

"Father," Niko said. "This alternative is the best option for Isabel. The choice of a husband should be hers."

"What's best for Isabel may not be what's best for Vernonia," his father countered.

"As Niko said, I believe this is best for Vernonia." Isabel spoke with no hesitation. "I've known Boyd for years. We enjoy the same things. People we know won't think it's weird if we eloped. They will believe we're married, not trying to trick them."

His father hesitated. "That means the Separatists would believe it, too."

She nodded. "If they thought my marriage was a ruse, we'd be no better off."

"Plausibility is important," his father agreed.

Finally. Progress. "So you agree, sir."

"Are you in love with this Boyd fellow?" his father asked.

"This is ridiculous." Niko stood, irritated and frustrated. "Love has nothing to do with the choice, Father. Please do not make this any harder on Isabel than it already has been."

His father frowned. "I will not tolerate outbursts

from you."

"I will stop when you cease toying with Isabel."

"Thanks, Niko." She smiled up at him, and his pulse quickened. "I appreciate you standing up for me, but I don't mind answering the question."

She sounded sincere.

Niko sat.

"I love Boyd, sir."

Isabel's words hit Niko like a left jab. An instant, squeezing pain overcame his chest. Something he'd never felt before.

Surprise.

That was what the feeling must be. She had not mentioned loving Boyd last night.

"A platonic love," she clarified, giving Niko instant relief. "Boyd is one of my closest friends. He's like a brother. There are no romantic feelings between us. The marriage would be in name only with the intention of divorcing when it was safe. For Vernonia and all parties involved."

Her clarification eased the tightness in Niko's chest. He envied Boyd for having such a relationship with Isabel. Niko had not experienced a close friendship with a man or a woman since the death of Stefan, who had been a big brother and best friend rolled into one. Now Niko's duty to Vernonia took precedence over everything and everyone else, including long-term romantic relationships. Short-term ones, too.

His father studied Isabel. "This is quite a sacrifice you are willing to make."

Isabel shrugged. "Not really, when you consider my parents and Uncle Frank gave their lives for me and Vernonia. I will be able to get involved in car racing, which is my dream, so I wouldn't call what I'm doing a sacrifice, sir."

His father beamed. "You've thought this through, Izzy. Well done."

Niko's admiration for her grew. "I agree."

She looked up at him.

Isabel's hazel eyes appeared to have a blue-green tint. Her jacket must be bringing out the color. The same gold flecks from last night were visible today, too.

Very pretty.

His father cleared his throat.

"I accept this alternative," his father proclaimed. "Isabel may marry Boyd."

"Yes!" Isabel pumped her fist. "Thanks, Dee. I mean, Your Highness. Majesty. Sir."

Not quite the perfect princess, but she was the perfect Isabel. Niko smiled.

"We will delay your appointment with the High Court until Tuesday to give Boyd time to arrive," his father said. "Have Jovan prepare the paperwork for the annulment, transfer of Aleksander's estate, and a marriage license."

"He's working on it, Father."

His father raised a brow. "Confident I would say

yes?"

"Hopeful," Niko admitted. That and he hadn't been able to sleep knowing how negatively this was affecting Isabel.

"Then we're set," his father said.

"Not quite, sir." Izzy stood, and Niko rose to his feet. "I still have to ask Boyd if he'll marry me."

His father chuckled. "He's a fool if he doesn't want to be your husband."

"Not only a fool." Niko liked the blush staining Isabel's cheeks a bright red. "A complete idiot."

"Well, I hope Boyd is neither of those things, but I'd better find out." She curtsied. "If you'll excuse me, sir."

As soon as she exited, his father grinned wryly. "I never thought there would come a day when I'd hear you admit to being not only a fool but also an idiot."

"I didn't."

"Not directly. But you *are* married to Izzy and don't want to be her husband."

"It's not the same situation," Niko protested. "Julianna brings a large dowry, one bigger than Isabel's inheritance, and Aliestlian trade support. Her royal pedigree will provide alliances with other European kingdoms, and she has the knowledge necessary to be queen. Even the Separatists support her. Isabel is an American, a mechanic. She doesn't know the first thing about being a princess or about Vernonia. She has no qualifications to be queen."

"Isabel is honest, loyal, smart, and has royal blood running through her veins," his father countered. "You say she is not qualified, yet this American mechanic is willing to marry someone she doesn't love for a country she hasn't stepped foot in since she was a baby, until twenty-four hours ago."

Each word stabbed at Niko like one of the soldier's bayonets on display at the National Museum. He stared at the floor.

"You may want to redefine what makes a queen, my son. Not only for your own sake, but your wife's. Otherwise you truly will appear foolish."

"Come on." Outside the castle, Izzy checked the reception bars on her cell phone. Nothing. She shook the phone. "What's a girl gotta do to get coverage around here?"

They weren't that far from town. A cell tower had to be around somewhere. She'd tried using a phone inside the castle but couldn't figure out how to get a dial tone. If only Niko were here...

Strike that. She didn't need his help or to have him make her heart go pitter-patter.

Izzy passed the garden and went down three steps.

Her eyes burned from exhaustion. The stone path hurt the bottom of her feet. Her fault. She'd ditched her uncomfortable shoes ten minutes ago. But she couldn't give up.

The king had given his approval. Now she needed Boyd's.

Time was ticking. Izzy needed to make this call. She checked the display. No bars. "I bet this place still uses dial-up internet connections."

"The castle has a wireless network," Niko said from behind her.

"What are you doing out here?" It was as if her thoughts had conjured him up like some magic wish. "I thought you had stuff to do."

"Yes, but I wanted to see if you reached Boyd."

"Not yet." She held up her lousy excuse for a cell phone. "No service."

He laughed. "So that's why you were threatening to feed your phone to the fish."

"I—" Okay, she had said that, but he hadn't been there. "How did you know that?"

"A gardener warned the staff about a barefoot American screaming at her cell phone." Amusement danced in Niko's eyes. "I thought it might be you."

Heat stole into her cheeks. "Jules said, when you're royalty, someone is always watching even if you can't see them."

"That is true."

"But I wasn't screaming," Izzy defended herself. "At least not that loud."

With a grin, he punched in numbers and handed

his cell phone to her. "It's a satellite phone. I put in the country code for America. You're all set."

"Thanks." She appreciated his help. It wasn't only loaning her the phone. He'd stuck up for her with his father this morning. If only Niko could make the call...

Nerves battered at her stomach. Her mouth felt as if cotton had been stuffed inside. She swallowed. This was her future, so much depended on the outcome of this call. She clutched the phone.

He rocked on his heels. "I can give you privacy."

"It's up to you."

"I'll stay."

Izzy figured he would because Niko took his responsibilities seriously. That included her even if she was his wife in name only. She punched in Boyd's number and held the phone to her ear. Niko watched her intently.

Izzy focused on the phone ringing. Once, twice, three times.

"Hello?" Boyd sounded sleepy, as if she'd woken him. "Who is this?"

Of course he wouldn't know Niko's number. "It's Izzy."

"Good to hear from you, Iz." His voice sounded stronger. "Is that prince dude treating you nice?"

"Yes, he's been a perfect gentleman." As her gaze met Niko's, her pulse skittered. "I'm, uh, calling you on his phone."

"I don't like the way he looks at you."

Izzy took in Niko's broad shoulders and athletic physique his suit couldn't hide. As his appreciative gaze traveled the length of her, heat rushed up her neck. "Don't worry about that, but..."

"What is it?" Boyd's voice sharpened.

She gripped the phone tighter. "I'm in a jam and need your help."

"You want my help?"

"You don't have to sound so surprised."

"Okay, but I am," Boyd said. "Doesn't matter, though. Whatever you need, my answer is yes."

"Wait to hear what I have to ask you." As Niko gave her a conspiratorial wink, her heart stuttered. "It, um, might change your answer."

She needed to focus. Something difficult to do with Niko around, but this was too important to let his gorgeous face distract her.

As Izzy studied a leaf on the ground, she explained to Boyd what had happened between the Separatists and the Loyalists in the past, what could happen, and how she had become drawn into the mess.

"So what do you need from me?" Boyd asked.

"It's a lot to ask, but I need a husband. Not forever. Just a few years." She took a deep breath. "Will you marry me, Boyd?"

As Boyd took his time answering, Niko watched Isabel. Her toes wiggled. She kept readjusting the phone at her ear.

The man was a fool for making Isabel wait so long.

Her face brightened. "Thanks, Boyd. You don't know what this means."

She laughed. The delightful sound floated on the air. "Okay, you're on."

On what? Niko would have liked to hear both sides of the conversation.

Izzy flashed him the thumbs-up sign. She was happy. Excellent. He should be feeling the same relief, not the regret and disappointment playing Ping-Pong inside him.

"I'll have Jovan call you with the travel details. You'll have to leave tonight." She bounced from foot to foot. "Yeah, I know. And Rowdy is invited. Duncan, too. I'll see you both tomorrow. Bye."

Izzy disconnected the call, ran to Niko, and threw her arms around him. "I don't have to marry a total stranger. Boyd said yes!"

As her soft curves molded against Niko, heat pounded through his veins.

She hugged him tightly. "Thanks."

Niko wasn't sure what he'd done to earn this reaction. He didn't care. He wrapped his arms around her, enjoying how she fit perfectly against him.

"We did it," she said.

"Yes." The scent of her hair tickled his nose. "We

did."

Isabel's face was so close. Her lips were parted. An invitation?

Niko wanted to press his mouth against hers. He wanted to know what her kiss tasted like. Sweet or tangy?

So tempting.

Longing that matched his own filled her eyes. With each breath she took, each beat of her heart, the truth became clear. She wanted him to kiss her.

Yet...

Julianna was ready to say "I do." Isabel was his wife, but another man had accepted her proposal. Anything they did would be wrong. Illicit. Hurtful to the two people they'd agreed to marry.

Niko lowered his arms and stepped out of her embrace.

Disappointment pinched her face. Her smile faltered. She handed him his phone. "I'm sorry for getting carried away with my celebrating."

"You do not need to apologize."

"If someone saw..."

"You are my wife. We hugged. That is not a crime."

"Yeah, a hug." She sounded resigned. "No big deal."

"Right." Though the embrace had felt like a bigger deal to Niko. He missed her touching him. Her warmth. The feel of her moist breath.

"Jules wants to work with me today." Isabel stared

at the ground. "Princess lessons."

He couldn't deny the chemistry between them, but kisses and more touches were complications he could ill afford. His feelings were strictly physical. They had to be because he hardly knew Isabel. "I have things to take care of myself."

"I'd better get going. I need to remember where I took off my shoes."

"If you can't find them..." Niko was about to offer to help her, but he couldn't. He needed to limit his time with her. "Ask one of the staff to assist you."

Izzy nodded. "See you later?"

She was a fair princess. And he didn't want her anywhere near him.

The words of—it might have been Shakespeare— swirled through Niko's head.

"Perhaps." Unless he could convince Julianna to join him for dinner after they sailed. He needed her to take his mind off Isabel. "Otherwise, I'll see you tomorrow at breakfast."

Chapter Twelve

Two hours later, Izzy walked across the library with a book on her head. Okay, "across" was a slight exaggeration. She traveled three steps before the book fell off and landed on the wood floor with a *thump*.

"I don't see why I need to do this." Izzy blamed her lack of concentration on not sleeping last night, but the real reason was Niko. She couldn't stop thinking about hugging him and wanting to kiss him. "No one will watch how I walk."

"Princesses need perfect posture," Jules said.

"But I'm not going to be a princess." Izzy held the

etiquette book she'd been balancing on her head. None of this stuff Jules was trying to teach her mattered. Not now, anyway. "I'm going to marry my friend Boyd and return to Charlotte. As long as I put my napkin in my lap at mealtime, I'll be good."

"Being good isn't enough. You must be the best. People have expectations. You must not disappoint them." As she spoke, Julianna proved why Niko wanted to marry her. "You are a princess no matter where you live."

"Yeah, but if someone calls me by my title, I might have to deck them."

Jules cringed. "Izzy..."

"I know." She sighed. "Princesses don't punch."

"You may fight if attacked."

What defined an attack? Since arriving in Vernonia, Izzy felt as if she'd gone nine rounds. She was exhausted, confused, and frustrated. Not to mention, attracted to her soon-to-be ex-husband and the soon-to-be husband of her new friend. "I just want to go home."

"I'm so sorry." Compassion filled Jules's voice. "I know exactly how you feel."

The beautiful princess who would marry the handsome prince and live happily ever after as they ruled Vernonia had no idea how Izzy felt. No one could. Still, she didn't want to be rude. Poor manners went against princess protocol. "Thanks."

Jules started to speak but then pressed her lips

together. Niko and King Dmitar used the same gesture. Maybe it was a royal thing, stiff upper lip and all that.

"I'm good. Really," Izzy added. "At least I get to pick who I marry, right?"

"Yes. You are fortunate in that regard." Jules removed a heavier book from a shelf. "Try again. Remember, shoulders back, chin up, and smile."

Multitasking at its finest. Izzy placed the book on her head. "I will have the best posture of any mechanic east of the Mississippi."

"That's the spirit." Jules checked her watch. "I'm going sailing with Niko. Would you like to come along?"

Izzy remembered the "faking her death by drowning" suggestion. She would like to go, but she didn't want to be a third wheel. Jules was the closest thing to a girlfriend Izzy had in Vernonia, yet she had wanted to kiss Niko. That went against princess protocol and the friendship code. She needed to distance herself from the prince.

"Thanks, but I need to practice." She repositioned the book on her head. "Then I want to take a nap."

"You could sleep on the boat," Jules offered. "We'll be going out to dinner afterward. It should be fun."

"Sounds like it, but no, thanks."

"You're sure?"

Was there a hint of disappointment in Jules's tone? No, Izzy had to be mistaken. The lovely princess was just clarifying her position.

You may fight if attacked.

She remembered Jules's firm handshake. Izzy had a feeling the princess could hold her own in a battle, especially if another woman hit on Niko. Not that Izzy would, but she didn't want to put Jules in an awkward position by intruding on their date. "I'm positive."

If Izzy repeated that enough times, she might come to believe it.

The next morning, Izzy ate alone in the breakfast area. That was what she called the smaller dining room because the only time it appeared to be used was for the first meal of the day.

Izzy took a bite of the cheese blintzes covered with a raspberry sauce and swallowed. Delicious.

Add yummy food to the list of princess perks.

Jules entered and sat opposite Izzy. The princess wore a stylish polka-dot, short-sleeve dress. Her hair fell loose past her shoulders.

"Good morning, Izzy." A uniformed server appeared and filled Jules's cup with coffee. "You seem more rested today."

"I am." Izzy had woken feeling more like herself. Her attraction to Niko was nothing more than a crush. Yes, he was gorgeous and had come to her rescue—so to speak—when her world was imploding yesterday. But things were clearer this morning. "A few hours of sleep can go a long way."

Common sense was also kicking in. She didn't want to be with a man who saw her as anything but an equal. Niko came from a different world and held a foreign viewpoint. Trying to be his equal would be impossible. They shared no common ground, other than a desire to annul their marriage. She had no rational reason to think about almost-kisses or dreamy blue-green eyes, did she?

Izzy sipped her freshly squeezed orange juice. "I hope you had a nice sail and dinner."

Despite knowing she was taking the right course of action with Niko, she squelched the pinprick of jealousy. She shouldn't be feeling that way, but she'd tried not to think of the two together out on the water. She'd mostly succeeded.

Izzy had more important things on her mind. Boyd arrived today. Tomorrow would be the biggest day of all. Her marriage would be annulled, she would receive her inheritance, and she would wed her coworker and friend. When they were in Charlotte, she would have more money than she ever imagined. That was nothing like the happily ever after Jules and Niko would share, but Izzy was more than satisfied with the outcome.

"I did. The sailing was very enjoyable. Thank you." Jules's face glowed. Another uniformed server placed a plate of food in front of the princess. "I love sailing.

There's nothing else I'd rather do."

"That's how I feel about car racing."

"We have more in common than you realize." The sincerity in Jules's voice wrapped around Izzy like a hug. "I hope you enjoyed your evening."

"I had dinner with the king and queen."

"And?"

Izzy recalled the conversation. Well, more like an inquisition, but the ruling couple had been so curious about her. "It was...interesting."

"How so?"

Her head and throat hurt thinking about all the talking she'd done. "They asked me so many questions I felt like a game show contestant."

Jules sipped her coffee. "What did they want to know?"

"Everything."

"Intriguing."

"They may have been trying to make me more comfortable. Put me at ease," Izzy admitted. "I had a couple mishaps."

Lines creased Jules's forehead. "Oh, dear."

Izzy laughed. "That's exactly what the queen said. After my third mistake, Queen Bea was laughing and wondering if *she* was using the correct fork or not."

"Laughter makes everything better."

Niko stormed into the room carrying a stack of newspapers. His lips were pressed together. His brows furrowed. "We have a problem."

Izzy had no idea what could put so much worry on a prince's face. Whatever the problem, it couldn't be good.

Jules set her fork on the plate. "What's happened?"

Niko unfolded the top paper and showed them the front-page. Isabel stared at her photograph. "That's me. What's the headline?"

"Princess Isabel Zvonimir Kresimir Lives!"

Jules gasped and then covered her mouth with her hands.

Izzy read her name in the unknown language with a strange sense of detachment. Seeing herself called a princess seemed surreal. As did having her first name paired with two different last names. "What does the article say?"

"It's a complete biography of you, including your return to Vernonia." He handed the bottom paper in the stack to Izzy. "Whoever leaked this information to the press will pay."

"It'll be okay. Boyd's on his way." Izzy wanted to put a positive spin on things. They had a plan. They didn't need to get distracted. "We knew my identity would come out at some point."

"We wanted to control when that happened." Niko tossed the rest of the papers on the table. "I gave you the English version."

Izzy read. Each time she came across *wife* or *bride*, she squirmed. The details in the story made the knot in the pit of her stomach grow. "Whoever leaked the information must have overheard my conversation with your parents last night."

Niko frowned. "We have never had any problems with the staff before."

"Some of the article quotes what I said. It's also kind of strange." Izzy scanned the article once more. "There's little about my life before I arrived in Vernonia. Your parents and I discussed my job at Rowdy's, but nothing is mentioned. This article makes me appear to have been living the life of an exiled royal hiding out in North Carolina, not a mechanic working at a garage trying to make ends meet."

"That is good," Jules said. "People will only see you as a princess."

Unease shot through Izzy. She straightened. "There's nothing wrong with being a mechanic."

"No," Jules admitted. "But as King Dmitar mentioned the other night, there's a perception."

Niko's frown seemed permanently etched on his face. "I would have rather they had called you a grease monkey than my wife or princess bride."

Izzy winced. Okay, that hurt. She referred to herself as a grease monkey—Boyd, too—but hearing Niko call her that with such condescension stung. Not knowing what to say, she stared into her coffee cup.

"I'm sorry, Isabel." Niko spoke quickly, but she didn't look at him. "That came out wrong. I didn't mean to hurt you."

She couldn't tell if he was contrite or not, but it

didn't matter. Things would be over soon. That gave her an idea. "Why don't we go to the High Court now, and then you won't ever have to hear me called either again?"

"I misspoke," he said. "I am sorry."

Izzy glanced his way.

"My apology is sincere." His cheeks had reddened. "The wording, especially the usage of husband and wife, in the article suggests a closer, more intimate relationship than what we have."

"The article is slanted. That's nothing new." Izzy couldn't wait to leave the country with Boyd and Rowdy. Vernonia wasn't bad, but this wasn't home. "But once the annulment—"

"Jovan is at the royal office in town," Niko interrupted. "People are assembling. The Separatist colors are flying in support of you. The people want you to be the next queen."

Her mouth gaped. "The people just found out about me."

His jaw thrust forward. "News travels fast."

"Talk to them," she implored him. "Tell them Jules will be your wife. Explain how I'm engaged to Boyd."

Jules's gaze met Niko's. Unspoken communication passed between them.

"I cannot," he said.

The sudden silence increased the tension in the room tenfold. Izzy had no idea what was going on. She struggled to put the pieces together.

The Separatists have wanted your bloodline to rule their portion of Vernonia.

Your father believed that a union between the two royal families would appease the Separatists and avoid war. His goal, our goal really, was to unite Vernonia with your marriage.

History has shown a marriage between rival sides can ease the strife and lead to peace.

I hope you aren't suggesting we remain married, sir.

Something clicked in Izzy's brain. She struggled to fill her lungs with oxygen. The weight of the people— a country—pressed on her chest, on her heart.

No. She was wrong. She had to be wrong. But the only way to find out was to ask. "Will there be an annulment?"

A muscle flicked at Niko's jaw. "The response by the Separatists this morning is similar to how the conflict began years ago."

Conflict. The anguish in his voice struck at her heart. What he meant was war. A bloody civil war that had killed her parents, his brother, and caused a nation to suffer.

"The High Court and my father will not allow an annulment now," he added.

Vernonians have quick tempers. Our loyalty is our strength, but our biggest weakness. We will cling to our causes until the bitter end. Whether right or wrong.

Izzy trembled. Emotions raged. "You mean, for now."

Regret shone on his face. "I mean, forever."

Niko snuffed out her spark of hope.

No annulment. He would remain her husband. She would stay...here. Her life, her dreams...

Staring at the table, she fought to remain in control. She couldn't lose it. And then she remembered. She wasn't the only one affected by this.

Guilt at her selfishness coated her mouth. Her gaze bounced from Niko to Jules. "What about the two of you?"

"A dowry can't stop a war. Only you can, Isabel." Niko spoke as if he were resigned to his fate. "None of us want this, but for the sake of Vernonia, will you consider remaining my wife?"

That was romantic. Not.

"This is crazy. Our marriage didn't stop the war twenty-three years ago." The words poured from her lips like steam from an overheated engine. "We don't know if us being married will work this time. We shouldn't be forced to give up our dreams for a what-if."

Niko's features sharpened with disdain. Tight lines bracketed his mouth. "I will not risk my country and my people so you can go back to America to play with race cars."

The abrupt change in him unnerved her, but she met his accusing expression without flinching. "I was talking about you and Jules."

"I'm okay with this, Izzy." Jules sounded encouraging, but that was her nature. The princess kept a tight rein on her emotions. She wouldn't show how she felt.

"Well, I'm not." Izzy stood. "The two of you are perfect together. You're in love. You should be able to marry."

"Isabel," Niko said. "You should know—"

"I know enough." The desperation in her voice matched the way Izzy felt inside. She might be attracted to Niko, but that wasn't enough reason to marry a man who didn't love her, a man who wanted to marry someone else. "This country is completely backward. I want nothing to do with it. Nothing at all."

She moved away from the table, not caring that her chair clattered to the floor, and ran out of the room.

Chapter Thirteen

Isabel disappeared before Niko could stop her.

Regrets assailed him. He had hoped she would calmly do what was required of her, not get emotional and run away. He needed to make her understand what was at stake. Trying to ease the tension knotting his insides, he flexed his hands.

But, he couldn't forget this wasn't only about Vernonia. Being forced to change her entire life would be difficult for Isabel. Of course she was struggling with this latest turn of events. Anybody would.

He was, too.

Even if he'd been taught to hide his turmoil.

He felt blindsided when he at least understood how things operated. Isabel must be reeling, and he'd done nothing to help her.

Niko hung his head. "That did not go well."

"She is young. An American." Julianna lowered her coffee cup. "All this is foreign to her."

He needed to remember that even though Isabel was royalty in Vernonia, she had no idea how things worked. She was making assumptions. Some wrong. "I'll go after her."

"Give her time."

"Isabel is upset. She shouldn't be alone." He'd hurt her by implying she was being selfish. He needed to explain about his relationship to Julianna. "It's my responsibility."

Julianna sighed. "Izzy is not a responsibility. She's a person. Your wife. A woman can tell if you're with her because you want to be or because you feel obligated."

"I *am* obligated." Frustration tightened the muscles in his neck and shoulders. "Isabel is not prepared to fulfill this role. Not the way you are."

"Isabel may not be a typical princess, but her heart is in the right place."

"She does not want to be my wife."

"She is upset and frightened. Your behavior only made her more so."

His jaw tightened. He didn't appreciate being

called out on his behavior even if he deserved it. "Isabel's feelings about arranged marriages are clear."

"I will stay and help her adjust," Julianna offered. "Perhaps if I do not go home, my father won't make another match for me right away."

Niko studied Julianna's face. Her eyes appeared brighter. Her complexion had more color. "You're happy with the way things have turned out."

"Not happy. I would never wish this upon dear, sweet Izzy. But I am...relieved," Julianna admitted. "No one should be forced to marry someone they do not love. No offense."

"None taken." This side of her surprised him. "Yet you agreed to the marriage."

He cringed. He sounded like his father.

She lifted her shoulder in a delicate shrug. "I was only doing what my father told me to do. What was expected of me. My royal duty. As I have done my entire life."

"I have always done the same thing."

She raised a finely arched brow. "Are you certain about that?"

Her question offended him. He squared his shoulders. "Everything I have done has been for Vernonia."

"If that's the case, why would your parents go to the press about Izzy?"

"My parents would never—"

"They were the only ones who could have

provided the information," Julianna interrupted. "While you and I were at dinner, they quizzed Izzy about her past. Her answers appear in the article. But isn't it strange how only positive information was published about her? The press rarely works that way."

I may not be a stickler for tradition, but I will always do what is best for the country.

As will I.

Niko's stomach knotted. "I need to speak with my father."

Julianna rose. "I'll find Izzy."

He appreciated her help and her friendship. "You would have made a fine queen for Vernonia."

"Thank you." She bowed her head. "I know you will be an excellent king, especially with Izzy by your side."

If only he believed that could be true...

As if on autopilot, Izzy followed the directions given to her by a butler. If she hadn't taken a wrong turn, the stone path should lead to the garage. That was the only building on the grounds where she might not feel so out of place, the only spot that might remind her of...home.

The tower loomed above Izzy as if mocking her. She grimaced. The castle no longer seemed part of a romantic fairy tale. It belonged in the pages of a terrifying Gothic novel.

Would she ever be allowed to return to Charlotte? If only for a visit? Or would she be forced to stay in Vernonia forever, married to a man who didn't want her for his wife?

Izzy's insides twisted. She might have found Niko attractive. She might have wanted to kiss him. She might have even dreamed about him, too. But Izzy couldn't fathom spending the rest of her life married to a husband she didn't love, a husband who didn't love her. Her stomach churned.

She stumbled on a rock. *Stupid heels*. Somehow she caught herself before falling flat on her face. Surprising, since she felt as if she were carrying two tires—the hopes and dreams of Vernonia—on her shoulders. She was about to collapse from the load.

Izzy kicked off her shoes to keep from falling again.

Up ahead was a rectangular brick building. That had to be the garage.

Welcome relief flowed through her. She quickened her pace and entered through the side door.

The smell of motor oil greeted her like a long-lost friend. Tears pricked, but she wasn't going to cry. If she started, she might not stop.

Izzy surveyed the interior: tools, tires, air compressor, an old truck, and a limousine. She leaned against a wall and slid to the cement floor.

Her shoulders slumped.

Izzy had no idea how long she sat there. She didn't care. Nor did she plan on leaving soon.

Here in the garage, she belonged. She couldn't say that about anywhere else in the castle, not even the bedroom where she slept.

A door on the opposite side opened. The sharp staccato of heels echoed through the garage until Jules stopped in front of Izzy. "Rough morning."

Staring at the truck in front of her, she nodded.

Jules sat next to her on the floor.

Izzy shot her a sideways glance. "You will get dirty."

"That'll make two of us."

"I don't mean to be rude, but I don't want to talk."

Jules wrapped her hands around her bended knees. "Then you can listen."

Izzy focused on the puddle of oil under the truck. Somebody needed to fix the leak.

"Niko and I aren't in love."

Her gaze jerked to Jules. "What?"

"Our marriage is an arranged match. My third, actually," Jules explained. "Arranged marriages are the tradition in Aliestle, whether you are a royal or a commoner. My first match was made when I was seven, but he was deemed unacceptable when I was a teenager. Too bad because I...liked him. I was twenty-five when the second one was arranged. My marriage to Prince Richard of San Montico would have realigned our two countries after one hundred and thirty-nine years of feuds, but he was in love with someone else and married her. And then came Niko. He's honorable. Respectful. Attractive. But I'm not in love with him, and he isn't in love with me."

Izzy stared in disbelief. "The two of you get along so well."

"We have common goals and a similar sense of duty."

"Duty?"

"I am a princess of Aliestle. My royal duty is to do what is best for my country even if it isn't something I may choose for myself."

"Like Niko."

Jules nodded. "I have no doubt my father will make a fourth match for me as soon as he learns what has happened here. But until then, I'm free and the feeling is glorious."

"I had no idea. I'm sorry." Compassion made Izzy reach out to her friend. "If I were you, I would have run away by now."

Jules laughed. "I imagine you would have, but this is the way I've been raised. Aliestle's customs are more archaic than Vernonia's. Our land is rich with natural resources so we can afford to be...eccentric and backward with our traditions."

"But to marry someone you don't love..."

"I have dreamed about marrying for love since I was a little girl." Jules sighed. "The reality, however, is an arranged marriage to best suit the needs of my country, especially if it means I might be a queen someday."

"Doing one's duty appears to be my new reality as a royal, and it sucks."

"Yes, sometimes it does," Jules admitted. "Duty and country first. But I'll tell you a secret. Even though I've known I would be told whom to wed, I've never given up hope that somehow I'll be able to marry for love. However remote the possibility."

"I hope it works out for you."

"Thanks, but I'm not holding my breath."

"It won't happen for me now."

"No, but Vernonia needs you, Izzy."

"Vernonia isn't my country."

"But it was your parents' country and your uncle Frank's."

Izzy hadn't been thinking about them. Only herself. That wasn't the way to honor the three people who had given up so much for her.

Guilt over her selfishness seared her heart. She needed to focus on what they would have wanted her to do in this situation even if it wasn't what she wanted. "I only wish staying married didn't feel so wrong. I wish...I loved Niko."

"But you have feelings for him, yes?"

"Maybe." That seemed the safest answer. "I've been on a roller-coaster ride since I met him in Charlotte. One minute, I'm a mechanic. The next, I'm a princess. I'm supposed to marry Boyd, now I can't. Things keep changing so fast I don't know what I feel for Niko."

"Just because you don't love someone at the beginning doesn't mean feelings won't develop. Love can grow."

"Do you really believe that?"

Jules smiled wryly. "Each time my father proposes another match, I hope it's true."

Izzy couldn't ignore the bigger piece in all this—Vernonia. People here, like those everywhere, deserved to live in peace. Her parents had wanted that. She believed her uncle Frank had wanted it, too. Izzy's dreams of car racing suddenly appeared childish in comparison. Even if the High Court would miraculously grant her an annulment, she might be needed in Vernonia. "Then I must hope it's true, too."

Niko stood in the king's office. Sweat beaded on his forehead and dampened the inside collar of his shirt. He clenched his hands, struggling to control his temper. It wasn't working. "I cannot believe you would betray me."

"I didn't betray you. I spoke to the press for one reason and one reason only—to protect Vernonia. The Separatists want Izzy to be the next queen. We can't improve Vernonia if we're having another civil war." His father's lips thinned. "One day you'll understand the difficult decisions a ruler must make."

"If I am to rule, you need to treat me like the crown prince, not a pawn."

His father frowned, appearing affronted. "I haven't—"

"You could have been honest about what needed to be done and explained your reasoning. Not manipulate the situation as you have." The words rushed out full of emotion and guilt at what his father's actions had done to two innocent women. "You have forced Isabel into a corner and hurt Julianna. Vernonia desperately needs the alliance with Aliestle. It's more than the dowry. The trade support and the influx of investment capital will enable us to modernize and make real progress to compete with other European nations."

"Julianna is wealthy and beautiful, and even though her country has Separatist ties, she cannot unite the people the way Izzy will."

"Unite the people?" Niko stared at his father in disgust. "Have you not seen the gathering this morning? The Separatists' colors are flying. It's history repeating itself. Isabel should be taken from Vernonia immediately."

"So you can marry Julianna."

"So Isabel will be safe. I fear for her safety. As should you."

His father gave him a speculative look. "You like her."

"Excuse me?"

"Izzy." Laughter laced her name. "I saw how you touched her yesterday. The way you stared into her eyes."

Uncomfortable, Niko shifted his weight between his feet. He may like her, but that didn't mean they should remain married. "I hardly know her. I'm concerned about her well-being because of your underhanded tactics. The protests—"

"Izzy is safe," his father interrupted. "You were a child the first time this happened and only remember the bad parts growing up. These gatherings are different from before. These are celebrations, my son. Unity. Finally."

Satisfaction sang in his tone.

Something more was going on here. Niko could feel it in his bones. Going to the press had only been one part of this. "Boyd, his father, and their attorney are on their way to Vernonia, but you never planned on allowing Isabel to marry Boyd."

"I never planned on allowing you to annul the marriage."

Niko took a step forward. "How dare you?"

"I am the king. I do what is necessary."

"Necessary?"

"As soon as I discovered Izzy was alive, I saw the opportunity at providing lasting peace for Vernonia. A united country for all regions and all people. That is what Prince Aleksander and I hoped would happen twenty-three years ago with your marriage. I doubted you would go along so I used the annulment as bait to get your cooperation."

Fury infused Niko. "You can't play with lives this way."

"You were fine marrying Julianna."

"It was my choice. I've been willing to marry with no preconceived notions of love," Niko said through clenched teeth. "But you've dragged Isabel into this with your machinations and lies."

His father shrugged. "The end is worth the means."

"No, Father. It is not." Niko squared his shoulders. "I have tried to fulfill Stefan's role and help make his goals for our country come true. I have also tried to live up to being crown prince and sacrifice for Vernonia, but you cannot continue to scheme and coerce a young woman into marriage. This type of action must stop. Now."

"A ruler must—"

Niko held up his hand, cutting off his father. "Be honorable in both thoughts and deeds. That is what you taught me. If Isabel refuses to remain married to me, I will support her decision, despite the dangers."

Panic flashed in his father's eyes. "You must convince her. Vernonia needs an heir as soon as possible. A baby with both royal bloodlines."

"A baby?" Niko nearly choked. "Isabel doesn't want to be my wife. I doubt she will go willingly into my bed."

"Your duty—"

"I know my duty, sir. I've always known what is expected of me. I will talk with Isabel, but unlike you, Father, I will not manipulate her into marriage. No trickery will be involved. Or expensive trinkets to sway her. The choice will be Isabel's. And hers alone."

Chapter Fourteen

Jules returned to the castle, but Izzy stayed in the garage. The oil leak bothered her. She wanted to repair the truck so she located the necessary tools and drained the remaining oil.

"You need a pair of coveralls or you will ruin your outfit."

At the sound of Niko's voice, Izzy's heart lurched. Pathetic.

She hated the way she responded to him. He was only being nice because Vernonia needed her.

Izzy focused on the engine. "A little grease on my

clothes won't hurt anything."

"I wonder what Tom Ford would say about that. Or any of the other designers you might be wearing."

Izzy had no idea who had designed her outfit. She remembered two fashion designers mentioned had been American to honor the country where she'd grown up. The rest were from Vernonia, who had learned their craft at the best houses in Paris and Milan. "You mean Henry Ford."

Niko laughed. "I believe these belong to you."

Dressed in a blue suit, white dress shirt, and yellow silk tie, with her shoes dangling from the crook of his fingers, he didn't belong in the garage. Out of place, yes, but as handsome as a model.

She wouldn't deny his physical appeal, but that didn't mean she would fall in love with him. Worse, what if she did and he didn't feel the same way?

No, she couldn't allow that to happen.

She bent over the truck's engine and focused on repairing the problem.

"I found one shoe in a bush and the other on the grass," he said.

"Keep 'em."

"They are not my size."

She couldn't help but smile. "I'm sure you can find someone else they fit."

"They fit you, Isabel." He set the heels on the floor next to her. "Perfectly."

Izzy bit back a sigh. Okay, he was making an effort.

The least she could do was meet him halfway. She straightened and stuck her foot in one shoe.

Niko kneeled to help her.

"I've got it," she said.

He stood, letting her put on the other herself.

She slipped on the second one.

"I am sorry for what I said earlier. For all of what's been happening," Niko said, his expression contrite.

"Me, too." She fought the urge to reach out to him. Self-preservation—not the grease on her hands—kept her from doing so. "I shouldn't have run out the way I did."

"You had every right." Niko's gaze darkened. "We have been pawns in my father's game. His agreeing to let you marry Boyd was a ruse to put his plans into action. He leaked the information about you to the press. He never intended to allow us to annul the marriage."

Dee had been so nice to her. The queen, too. "Why would he do that?"

"To unite Vernonia. That is his goal as king. It's the same goal he shared with your father when they had us marry."

Her father. Izzy's chest tightened.

"What do you want to do?" Niko asked.

"There's a choice?" She'd been trying to resign herself to her fate since talking with Jules.

Deep lines bracketed each side of his mouth. "I hate what my father has done. I won't force you into…"

"Marriage?"

He nodded. "I told you the first day we met I wouldn't lie to you. I don't want to coerce you into remaining my wife."

Izzy appreciated that, except... "I'm not what you want for Vernonia."

"No." His confirmation, though honest and expected, jabbed her heart like a knife. "But you are what the country needs. Part of being a princess or a prince is putting your people first."

"Royal duty."

"Yes."

Niko believed that wholeheartedly. Jules, too. Izzy understood the necessity of peace, but not this "duty" they kept mentioning. The idea made her uneasy about the present and especially the future.

How would Izzy know if Niko came to care about her or if he was doing his duty, what he'd been doing since they met? She wouldn't. The answer unsettled her as much as the thought of unrequited love.

Still, she appreciated his leaving the decision up to her even if she really didn't have a choice.

"I don't like what your father did, either, but I will remain your wife. For Vernonia," she clarified, not wanting him to get the wrong idea.

"Thank you." He sounded relieved, but the tension on his face remained. "You are giving up your dreams for a land foreign to you."

"Keeping peace is more important. I couldn't live

with myself if I was the reason people were hurt or killed." She fiddled with a hose clamp to keep her hands busy. "I only hope your father is more honest and open in the future or things will be...difficult."

"I spoke with him about the future." Niko seemed hesitant, uncertain.

"And?"

"My father believes Vernonia needs an heir. He wants one as soon as possible."

Her stomach knotted. "This will be a, uh, real marriage?"

"I am the crown prince." A small smile played at the corners of Niko's lips. "An heir and a spare are the minimum for any royal marriage. Real or not."

Blinking, she forced herself to look away, but that didn't stop heat from creeping up her neck. "Can't a person get used to one thing before having something else thrown at her?"

He placed his hands on her shoulders.

Warmth, delicious and oh-so inviting, emanated from the point of contact. The entire dynamics of the situation seemed to change with the one touch. She focused on *seemed*. Their marriage was nothing more than a business arrangement with a total stranger—one who cared more about duty and country than anything else, including her.

"This is not the kind of marriage you planned on having with Boyd," Niko said. "But we will make this work."

"How?" Izzy wished she shared his confidence. "It's not as if we will fall madly in love with each other."

"No, this isn't a love match, but that doesn't mean we can't have a successful union."

"Successful?"

"Providing heirs."

"So it's all about the baby-making."

"Children are a goal."

"I appreciate your honesty, but maybe you could sugarcoat the truth, because faking my death appears to be a viable alternative now."

"You need to know what you're getting into." Niko spoke as if he were an employer offering her a job, not a husband talking about their relationship.

"Do we live together?" she asked. "I'm not sure how a marriage like this works."

"We have two options. A state marriage where we live as husband and wife until we have the required number of heirs, then we live our separate lives, only appearing together at state functions and for our children's sake."

Izzy wasn't expecting a fairy-tale ending, but she hadn't been prepared for something so...calculated. Her stomach roiled. She took deep breaths to keep from losing it.

A minute passed. Maybe two.

"Would I be able to live in Charlotte?" she asked finally.

He hesitated. "Possibly, but a divorce would never

be allowed and custody arrangements might be tricky."

Niko meant children, yet they'd never kissed. But she would never leave behind a child to move elsewhere. "What's the other option?"

"We live as husband and wife until death do us part."

"A together forever kind of thing?" she asked.

"As close to that as we could manage without being in love. Arranged marriages can be successful. Why shouldn't ours be? We like each other. That will be enough. Besides, marriages based on love don't come with any guarantees. Many people end up separating. Divorcing. Every marriage takes work if it's going to last."

"What kind of work?" she asked honestly. "I've never had a serious relationship before."

"Me neither," he admitted. "We will have to figure out what we need to do together."

Izzy rested her palms on the car. A marriage based on respect and honesty wouldn't be bad. "If we can't figure it out, we can always live apart."

A vein throbbed at his jaw. "If the marriage works..."

"Then we'll owe your father a big thank-you."

But the expression on Niko's face told her that would take a miracle. She shouldn't be surprised because he wanted to marry Jules, a woman completely opposite from Izzy.

He rocked on his heels. "It's settled."

"Not yet." Izzy straightened. "I don't see how we can make a marriage work when I don't feel married."

"We are married."

"I saw the photograph and the marriage certificate, but I was so young. I don't remember anything. Maybe if we had a wedding ceremony, one we both remembered, I'd feel like your wife."

He searched her face. "This is important to you."

"To feel married. Yeah, especially if we're going to, um..."

Amusement twinkled in his eyes. "Have sex."

This was *so* not what she wanted to be talking about with him. "Provide Vernonia with an heir."

"Do you enjoy sex, Isabel?"

Oh, man, he assumed she'd had sex. What was she going to say?

"I..." She looked around as if the answer would pop up on the engine or headlight for her to see. Of course, it didn't. Where was an enchanted castle when a person needed one? "I don't know. I've never..."

She couldn't finish the sentence. He might be her husband, but the thought of admitting her inexperience embarrassed her.

"Never?" he repeated, sounding intrigued.

"Never." She shifted positions, feeling self-conscious. "I had the chance, but I thought having sex after the first or second, even the third date was selling myself short. Uncle Frank said sex should be an expression of love and commitment, not a way to cap off dinner and a movie.”

Niko said nothing.

She flushed. “I don’t know how to be a princess. And I have no clue how to, um... I’m a total freak, aren’t I?”

“You are not a freak. My youth was nothing but war. When Stefan died, I was thrust into an unexpected role. I’m far from one of the playboy princes mentioned in the tabloids and on gossip internet sites.” His face flushed. “I have had limited...encounters with women. We will learn together.”

Not feeling so alone, she breathed a sigh of relief.

He reached out to tuck a strand of hair behind her ear. “You are beautiful.”

She shivered at the light touch. If only she felt beautiful.

“Do not worry. We have not known each other long, but there is chemistry between us,” he said in a husky tone.

Okay, he’d felt it, too. That had to count for something. Would it be enough?

He moved closer. “I didn’t try to discover more because of Julianna.”

“That was honorable of you.”

Wicked laughter gleamed in his eyes. “But now that it is only the two of us, and you are my wife...”

Izzy stepped back until she hit the truck’s bumper. “I wanted to kiss you the other night in the kitchen. Outside near the garden yesterday, too. But now, I don't want to do anything until I feel married."

He raised a brow. "Not even kiss?"

Temptation flared. A touch made her all tingly. A kiss might send her over the edge. "No."

"We shall have a wedding." His smile crinkled the corners of his eyes, and her heart beat like a timpani. "A royal wedding complete with a fanfare of bugles, a packed cathedral, and a horse-drawn carriage that would make Cinderella envious."

"That sounds elaborate." *And overwhelming.* "I was thinking a quick trip to the courthouse."

"You need to think bigger. Is there anything you want to have at your wedding?"

Izzy never had considered her wedding day, never daydreamed about it, or checked out wedding boards on Pinterest. "A white dress, maybe."

"That can be arranged."

"I want Rowdy and Boyd to be a part of the wedding. They're family."

"Fine."

She couldn't think of anything else… Until she thought of Uncle Frank and his favorite dessert. "I also want a tiered wedding cake with flowers made from buttercream icing, not that fondant stuff. I also want one cake to be chocolate."

"I shall place the requests myself." He sounded pleased, as if doing these small things were a much bigger deal than they were. "Anything else?"

What did she need as the bride—old, new,

borrowed, blue? Jules could help her with that. "No."

"If you think of something, please let me know and I'll make the arrangements."

"Thank you."

He tilted his head. "A wedding is a good start, but it is not enough. We shall go on a honeymoon."

Every single nerve ending stood at attention. She balled her hands so tightly her nails poked into her palms. A honeymoon implied romance, intimacy, sex. "That isn't necessary."

"We need to get to know each other and start our marriage correctly."

And conceive an heir.

The words were unspoken, but they might as well have been shouted for all of Vernonia to hear.

Her stomach sank. If a child—or children—was all Niko wanted, their marriage didn't stand a chance of succeeding.

Chapter Fifteen

At precisely one o'clock in the afternoon the following Saturday, a flourish of trumpets announced the royal wedding procession. As fifteen hundred guests, including Duncan Moore who had accompanied Boyd and Rowdy to Vernonia, sat in the intricately carved wooden pews, the ancient stone cathedral's walls swallowed the music.

An omen or poor acoustics?

Standing in the vestibule, Izzy shivered with apprehension.

The first of twelve bridal attendants, all wearing

ice-blue strapless silk gowns, strolled into the church. She'd barely met any of the women, but at least Jules was her maid of honor.

Even though I've known I would be told whom to wed, I've never given up hope that somehow I'll be able to marry for love. However remote the possibility.

Jules had received another reprieve from the altar. She'd also convinced her father to support trade with Vernonia and offer investment capital to assist their rebuilding efforts. Izzy hoped the princess's generosity would be rewarded and she would be allowed to marry for love.

It was too late for Izzy, but the relationship between her and Niko was improving. He'd made sure the royal wedding came together in less than a week and whatever she wanted on her wedding day happened. She'd been on her best behavior, trying to learn all she could about being a princess from Jules.

Would trying be enough to make a marriage work?

Izzy hoped so because she clung to the idea of love growing over time. That they could have a forever kind of marriage, not a state one.

Music continued to play. Izzy recognized the song. Soon she would be the one to walk down the aisle.

She remembered her princess instructions.

Shoulders back. Chin up. Smile.

Izzy could do this. She was a princess of Vernonia even if she was also a mechanic from Charlotte. She was getting married for her new country. For her parents. For Uncle Frank.

And Niko.

Her chest tightened.

He stood at the front of the church, waiting for her. Jovan, the best man, stood next to him and then came Boyd.

The only time she'd seen her friend in a suit was at Uncle Frank's funeral, but the tuxedo looked good on Boyd, even if he kept shifting positions. He was taking everything in stride, being the friend he'd always been. When she'd explained how she would be marrying Niko instead, Boyd had given her a strange smile and a shrug. If the change of plans had hurt him, he hadn't showed it. The king offering to buy Boyd a new truck for his troubles probably helped.

The woman coordinating the wedding motioned to an attendant.

Izzy exhaled. Not her turn. Yet.

The youngest daughter of a former Separatist leader entered the church through the massive arched doorway. The crowd's oohs and aahs floated on the air as if they were watching a fireworks display. The flashing of the camera bulbs and the web of electrical cords from the television crews made the wedding seem more like a sports event. Selling the television rights to the royal nuptials of the crown prince to the half-American princess had brought in more money than expected.

Rowdy cleared his throat. He stood next to her

ready to escort her down the aisle. Sweat beaded on his forehead. He seemed uncomfortable in the tuxedo. "You sure about this, Izzy?"

No. But then she pictured Niko. He'd been honest about his reasons for marrying her. He'd been open about the need for heirs and the types of marriages they could have. She'd also noticed the tenderness on his face when she caught him looking at her, the way he'd helped her since arriving, wanting her input on the wedding, and the love he had for his country. All those things told her he was a good, honorable man.

Izzy peered through the lace veil covering her face. In her shoe was a lucky coin Uncle Frank had always carried. Maybe it would bring her luck during her marriage.

She lifted her chin. "I'm sure."

Rowdy's eyes gleamed. "All your uncle Frank wanted was for you to be safe and happy."

"I am. Honest."

"Then we're good to go." Her ex-boss sniffled. "You're a beautiful bride."

"Thanks, Rowdy." Izzy felt pretty, even though she'd had plenty of help to prepare for the nuptials. Since early this morning, she'd been fussed over, primped, and pampered with a massage, manicure, pedicure, and expert makeup application. Jules had overseen and supervised everything. Three hairdressers had spent over an hour sweeping Izzy's hair up and through the diamond tiara that secured the cathedral-length veil. The last of the crystals and pearls had been hand-sewn on the bodice of her wedding gown only an hour ago by a dress designer, who'd been flown in at Julianna's request.

Yes, the crew of wedding experts had transformed Izzy into a fairy-tale princess bride even though she'd been the prince's wife for the past twenty-three years. The exchange of "I dos" didn't guarantee a happily ever after. She had no idea what to expect with the marriage. The birth of heirs would classify the match as a success or a failure, but would the union be full of love or loveless? That was the big question. One that wouldn't be answered for...years.

But maybe she was reading too much into this. Did any bride know how a marriage would turn out? All she could do was hope for the best. And would.

Two more attendants made the long walk down the aisle. In the vestibule, the remaining bridesmaids and six flower girls moved forward. Izzy had met them five days ago at a luncheon thrown by the wives of Parliament members.

Nerves escalating, Izzy gripped her all-white rose bouquet. She focused on the flowers' sweet fragrance.

Three more attendants made their way down the aisle. The folds of their gowns swished like flags in the wind.

Shoulders back. Chin up. Smile.

Jules flashed her a thumbs-up before stepping into the church. The six flower girls, dressed in layers of white ruffles, played with the white rose petals in their baskets. One, the youngest daughter of a duke, giggled.

The tight-faced, headpiece-wearing wedding coordinator shushed her. "Quiet. It's almost your turn."

Izzy would follow.

Her pulse rate doubled. She took a calming breath. Another. And another. But nothing settled her nerves.

Arranged marriages can be quite successful. Why shouldn't ours be?

She clung to what Niko had said, hoping they could spend the rest of their years together, not apart and married in name only.

The flower girls skipped into the church.

"It's almost time, ma'am," the wedding coordinator said.

Izzy's heart slammed against her chest. Each fierce beat reminded her of the cannon being shot off during the royal orchestra's performance of Tchaikovsky's "1812 Overture" at the Royal Hall on Tuesday night.

Another flourish of trumpets sounded. Rather, bugles, as Niko had called them. The signal. Her signal.

"Ready?" Rowdy asked.

Izzy would never be ready for this.

Behind her, two royal guards stood on either side of the massive wooden church doors. The instinct to run had never been stronger. But where would she go? What would she do? And who would clean up the mess she left behind?

She might not be a fairy-tale princess locked in a tower, but she was a prisoner of circumstance, as was Niko. The two of them were stuck with each other. Better just make the best of it.

Shoulders back. Chin up. Smile. "I'm ready."

Rowdy kissed the top of her hand. "You're the daughter I never had. I'm proud of you. I know Frank would be, too."

Tears stung her eyes. Rowdy's words filled her with warmth. "Thank you. Thank you so much."

She took hold of his arm. Somehow she lifted her heavy feet and stepped into the church without tripping on her gown and falling on her face.

Dignitaries, royalty, and movie stars stood to watch her, but the faces blurred. She focused on the altar.

Her steps faltered, but thanks to Rowdy's strong arm, no one noticed.

Shoulders back. Chin up. Smile. And breathe.

Izzy needed to breathe or she would faint.

The king and queen sat in the front pew, seeming more pleased than she'd seen them before. Izzy tried not to let that upset her.

When she reached the altar, Rowdy removed his arm from hers.

A tidal wave of doubt and apprehension surged through her. Izzy clutched the bouquet's handle so hard it bent.

Rowdy squeezed her other hand.

The gesture reassured her. He placed her hand into

Niko's.

She studied his neatly trimmed nails, smooth skin, strong hand. A husband's hand. The father of her children's hand.

His fingers clasped around hers. Tingles shot up her arm.

Breathe. Just breathe.

Slowly, her gaze traveled to his sleeve—a gold-braided cuff against black—and up his arm. He wasn't wearing a tuxedo, but a uniform with a light blue sash, one of the colors from the Vernonian flag, worn diagonally across his chest. A thin row of white from his shirt collar showed at the top of the jacket. Ribbons and medals decorated the left side. He wore a thin gold belt around his waist.

He looked like a prince from the movies. Long, thick lashes framed familiar blue-green eyes. His straight nose complemented high cheekbones. Full lips contrasted with the sculpted planes of his face. A mane of brown hair fell to his wide shoulders.

His smile softened his rugged features. Even his scar.

Tingles formed in her stomach.

Niko was too beautiful for a man, for a mere mortal. Yet here he stood as if crafted by the angels in Heaven especially for her. Her heart sighed.

And that was when Izzy knew.

There was only one reason she'd agreed to remain married to Niko. He might not be Prince Charming, but that didn't matter.

This might not be a love match for Niko, but it was becoming one for her.

She was falling for her husband. And falling hard.

Standing in the cathedral holding Izzy's hand, Niko's doubts quadrupled. His people had rallied around the young American, but she wasn't the princess bride he'd been expecting.

Wanted.

All his hopes and dreams for modernizing Vernonia had rested on his marriage to Julianna. She, however, was the maid of honor, not his bride.

"The veil," Jovan whispered.

Oh, right. Niko was supposed to lift Isabel's veil.

He released her hand and held on to the delicate lace with his fingertips. Slowly he raised the fabric, and...

The air whooshed from his lungs.

She was beautiful.

Gorgeous.

The most stunning bride he'd ever seen.

With her brown hair artfully arranged around a diamond tiara, she was the epitome of what a princess should look like. Her elegant white gown accentuated her curves and ivory complexion.

But beyond her appearance, Niko recognized her resolve and what she was giving up. She did not understand why royals embraced their duty as if it were a piece of their being—part of their hearts—but Isabel stood at the altar, sacrificing herself for the good of his country. Vernonia wasn't her country yet. It might never be.

That was when he knew.

She might not be Julianna with a treasury-sized dowry and connections, but Isabel would be a better princess—queen—than he believed she would be. He wanted to make this marriage work. Not only for Vernonia's sake but for hers and his, too.

We will have to figure out what we need to do together.

But how?

Niko had no idea what marriage would be like. He'd never had a serious girlfriend. His best friend had been his older brother, Stefan, who had kept Niko out of trouble and saved his life on at least two occasions. He didn't know how to create a successful marriage, but he didn't want to fail her.

He couldn't.

She stared up at him as if he were the sun, moon, and stars rolled into one. He could barely breathe. No one had ever looked at him that way.

It had to be the emotion of the moment. Or her makeup.

Isabel came to this marriage out of duty, the same as him. She had an escape route planned.

If we can't figure it out, we can always live apart.

Even if many of his peers quietly separated once they had provided heirs, he hoped their marriage didn't come to that.

The archbishop spoke.

Niko focused his attention on the celebrant, concentrating on the opening prayer. He'd been too young to remember his first wedding ceremony. He wanted to pay attention to this one. Unlike Isabel, he doubted an exchange of vows would make him feel more married. Only time and possibly a child would do that.

But no matter how he felt, Niko would put Vernonia first. He would do his duty as a prince and as a husband. Nothing less would be acceptable.

Izzy might be a continent away from home, but the ceremony was similar to weddings she'd attended in Charlotte. The unexpected sense of familiarity provided comfort—the last thing she expected to feel today.

Staring at Niko's handsome face, Izzy listened to the archbishop's words—love, honor, until death do you part.

"I do," she said when he'd finished speaking.

Niko released a quick breath.

Relief, she hoped. Not regret.

Izzy knew exactly what she wanted from this union. A real marriage. The together forever kind. But for that to happen, Niko would have to fall for her the way she was falling for him.

"Do you have the rings?" the archbishop asked.

Niko handed them over and then he repeated the necessary words.

Izzy prayed what he said would come true.

He slid a beautiful wide diamond-and-ruby-encrusted gold band on her ring finger. A perfect fit.

She ran her fingertip along the gold band she would give him. The royal historian claimed the diamond, ruby, emerald, and sapphire cross heirloom not only provided protection but also brought truth to light. Those two things had made choosing this wedding ring from the royal family collection an easy decision.

She gripped the band, afraid she might drop it. "I give this ring as a token of my love and fidelity."

With only the slightest tremble of her hand, she slid it onto his finger. Once again, a perfect fit.

The archbishop declared them husband and wife. "You may kiss your bride."

Their first kiss.

Izzy tensed from a mix of nerves and anticipation. Not to mention, the guests in the pews.

As Niko lowered his mouth to hers, she closed her eyes, remembering how much she'd wanted him to kiss her in the kitchen just over a week ago. *Or had it been a lifetime ago?*

His lips brushed hers and disappeared.

That was it?

Izzy pushed aside her disappointment and opened her eyes. She thought Niko had wanted to kiss her.

Suddenly his mouth returned, pressing against her lips. Hard, demanding, as if seeking her very soul. His urgency and need frightened yet excited Izzy. She'd never been kissed like this, and she never wanted the moment to end.

She used every ounce of willpower to keep from clinging to him. No matter how she might want to surrender to the feelings coursing through her, she couldn't forget where she was and who was watching. Not only the guests sitting in the pews but also a television audience viewing the ceremony from home.

Niko drew away slightly. His warm breath tickled her ear. "I cannot wait for tonight."

Anticipation buzzed through her. Izzy moistened her thoroughly kissed lips before glancing at the diamond ring on her finger.

She couldn't wait until later, either.

The reception passed in a blur. The guests seemed to enjoy themselves with the free-flowing champagne and mouthwatering food. Or "cuisine" as the queen called it.

Unbelievably, Izzy felt like a princess. She floated across the dance floor, whirling and twirling to the orchestra, with Niko's strong arms around her. He stayed at her side the entire time, introducing her to so many diplomats and dignitaries she couldn't remember their names. Rarely did he let go of her hand. She felt special, cherished, and that eased some of her nerves about what would happen later.

She was excited about their wedding night but worried about being alone with him. She didn't want to make a mistake.

After cutting the cake, Izzy stood at the railing of the landing between two sets of curved staircases for the bouquet toss. Izzy held onto the handle of her white rose bouquet. She saw anticipation on the women's faces below.

"Is something wrong?" Niko asked, his low voice seeping through her like warm caramel sauce.

"No." She remembered being one of the single ladies called to the dance floor at a mechanic's wedding last summer. No matter their station in life, royal or commoner, women wanted to catch the bouquet. She'd caught the flowers and laughed it off. Guess Fate had been right. "Just taking it all in."

"Savor the moment," Niko whispered. "But you may want to put the women out of their misery sooner rather than later."

Isabel turned away from the railing. On three, she let the flowers soar into the air behind her. She whipped around.

Women reached for the flowers. A few missed by

mere inches. The petals grazed another's fingertips. The bouquet landed in Jules's hands. The lovely princess stared at the roses in wide-eyed dismay and promptly dropped them.

Izzy laughed, but no one else seemed amused.

The wedding coordinator rushed to Jules's side, scooped up the bouquet, and handed them to the stunned princess. The royal photographer corralled Jules for a picture with the bride.

Izzy posed for the camera. "You're smiling, but you don't appear happy."

"Catching the bouquet might be a sign," Jules admitted. "I fear I may find myself matched to another royal in need of a wife before I return home to Aliestle."

The camera flash made Izzy blink. "Stay in Vernonia."

Jules sighed. "I wish I could."

"I'm serious." This seemed to be the best way for Izzy to help her friend. "We're spending tonight at the castle, but then we leave on our honeymoon. The king and queen won't mind. They enjoy having guests."

"My father might mind."

"Think about it," Izzy urged.

"I will." Jules hugged her. "Thank you."

Hours later in the suite that was the bedroom Izzy now shared with her husband, servants helped her out of her wedding gown. One thought kept running through her head. Wasn't a husband supposed to undress his wife on their wedding night?

Mare combed out Izzy's hair. Another woman ran a warm bath. A third lay out Izzy's peignoir set. The lovely confection of thin white fabric, lace, and ribbon had been a gift from Jules.

Izzy appreciated the women's efforts. They were only doing their jobs, but what was next? A mug of warm milk and a plate of cookies?

The most important person was missing. When a husband blew off his wife on their wedding night, the future of their marriage didn't bode well. She didn't need others here to add to her growing anxiety.

"Thanks for your help." Izzy could put on her own nightgown. "But it's been a busy day. Relax and enjoy the rest of the night."

The women left the room.

After bathing, she tied the satin ribbon on the robe for the third time. The bow was still lopsided. She gave up. Maybe Niko wouldn't notice.

Where was he?

Izzy paced barefoot across the large room. A television hung on the wall. Books filled nearby shelves. But she wasn't interested in watching TV or reading.

I cannot wait for tonight.

What he'd said during the ceremony had been playing in her head for hours. The flames on the lit candles around the room flickered. Shadows danced. A dance for one.

He was coming to their room, wasn't he?

Izzy walked to the French doors, opened them, and stepped onto the balcony. Stars twinkled in the inky sky. A breeze, carrying the scent of roses from the garden below, ruffled her hair and nightgown.

This was her new home.

She wanted to be with her new husband.

Tears pricked her eyes, but she would not cry even if Niko didn't seem to want to be with her.

Chapter Sixteen

Niko entered his suite carrying the bride box. He placed the wedding gift on the table next to two crystal flutes and a bottle of champagne chilling in a silver bucket. The box belonged to Isabel once again. The archaic custom had been fulfilled. He only hoped she felt like his wife now. If not, he would do his best to make sure she did by morning.

He was prepared.

Nervous, but he was ready.

The kiss during the ceremony had whetted his appetite and made him want to skip the reception, but that would have broken protocol, upset his parents, and dishonored dignitaries and guests.

The staff had decorated the room per his instructions. Soft music played. Flickering candles provided a romantic atmosphere. Someone had turned down the duvet and sheets so he could carry his virgin princess bride to their bed.

All he needed was Isabel.

Desire led him to the bathroom in search of her, but she wasn't there. Niko removed his belt, sash, and jacket. He also kicked off his shoes and pulled off his socks.

When he returned to the bedroom, it was still empty. That left...

Niko strode to the balcony doors. His sense of purpose belied anything he'd felt about her—about any woman—before. Isabel consumed his thoughts. She invaded his dreams. Maybe after tonight that would stop. He hoped so because he didn't like being so distracted.

He opened a door quietly.

A vision in white with a starry sky as her backdrop, she stood on the balcony, facing away from him.

His heartbeat sped up.

The breeze toyed with the ends of her hair the way his fingers longed to do. The fragile fabric of her long robe and matching nightgown ruffled around her legs.

Niko wanted to make tonight, their wedding night, special for Isabel. They might have been married for twenty-three years, but they would unite as husband and wife for the first time. He wanted her to enjoy the physical side of their marriage, not see sex as only an obligation to provide heirs to the kingdom. That could go a long way in making their marriage successful.

He stepped onto the balcony. "Wishing on a star or reconsidering faking your death?"

"I must admit drowning isn't looking too bad, but now that my wish has come true I might have to stick around longer." She turned with an expectant expression on her face. "What took you so long, Highness?"

Niko inclined his head. "I was forced to play polite with too many heads of state. I apologize for my delay, Highness."

She stared down her nose at him, but even ten feet away, her desire was unmistakable.

Anticipation sizzled. His blood heated and thrummed through his veins.

"I assume you will make it up to me," she said coquettishly.

Her unexpected playfulness thrilled him. "I won't stop until you are satisfied."

She came toward him but not close enough to touch.

The breeze lifted the ends of her hair again, brushing several strands across her face. His fingers itched to tuck the wayward strands behind her ear.

To touch her.

Isabel's bare feet carried her closer until the light from the bedroom bathed her. He glimpsed her silhouette through the sheer fabric.

"Promises, promises," she teased.

"I promise you will have no complaints, milady."

His words earned him a breathtaking smile. She reached for the satin ties on her gown. Her fingers fumbled. Not as cool and collected as she appeared to be. That endeared her more to him.

He longed to undress her, but he would give her more time.

"Allow me." Niko tied the two pieces of ribbon into a neat bow. "There."

Appearing confused, she stared at him through her thick lashes. "Aren't you supposed to untie it?"

"I didn't know we were in a hurry."

She flushed.

"Impatient?" he asked.

"Well, yeah." Isabel tilted her chin. "Given you're only wearing your shirt and pants, not the full uniform, I figured you were ready for the green flag so we could start the race."

"You want to race through tonight?"

"I mean—"

Smiling, he swept her into his arms and cradled her snugly.

She inhaled sharply. "What are you doing?"

Soft, feminine curves pressed against him. His body tingled with awareness. "Carrying you over the threshold."

"You claim not to be a fan of traditions and customs."

"A few have their place." He headed to the door. "Especially on our wedding night."

She trembled. "Okay, the nerves are kicking in."

He held her tighter. "Better?"

"Yes." Isabel ran her fingertip along his cheek. She shifted against him, stretching until she pressed her lips against the side of his face, against his scar. "So beautiful."

"Not as beautiful as you."

"I had help."

"Believe me, you need no assistance."

He didn't want to rush her, but being patient was difficult. Unable to resist the temptation in his arms, he lowered his mouth to hers. She arched to meet his kiss.

With no archbishop, no audience, and no cameras watching, Niko did what he'd wanted to do at the cathedral—take his time. No racing to the finish line tonight.

He savored her kiss, lingering and enjoying. She tasted sweet and warm with a hint of chocolate, like fondue. The castle chef used to make the rich chocolate fudge sauce for Niko's birthday each year. As he'd done when he was younger, he soaked up the taste.

Niko used his shoulder to push open the door as Isabel's eager lips pressed against his. Testing, tasting, hungry. Her arms circled around him. One hand combed through his hair. The other splayed against his back, between his shoulder blades, pressing him forward.

Nothing else mattered but Isabel.

Sensation swirled through Niko.

She wanted this. Wanted him.

Heat flared.

The kiss deepened.

Exploded.

Niko moved toward the bed, never letting his lips leave hers. He couldn't get enough of her kiss, of her. But he had to stop. He lifted his mouth from hers.

Isabel's eyes opened, her gaze hot and languid, intense and soft. A mass of contradictions. Just like her, his mechanic, his princess.

His *wife*.

He struggled to remain in control. He wanted to dispense with the niceties and abandon decorum. But, he needed to go slow, not overwhelm her with tangled limbs and sweaty skin.

Carefully, gently, he lowered her to the foot of the bed so she was sitting on the edge. He stood in front of her, watching her. Waiting for her to look away in shyness.

Her gaze never wavered from his.

Talk about a turn-on.

His chest tightened. His control slipped a notch. Maybe three.

Niko tugged on a ribbon to undo the bow he'd tied

on the balcony. He pushed the chiffon robe off her shoulders and down her arms until it fell over her hands and onto the bed.

He bent over, kissing her bare shoulder and showering more kisses along her neck and jaw.

Izzy tilted her head, giving him better access to her graceful neck. He continued kissing her. He loved the taste of her skin. His mouth grazed her earlobe.

A soft moan escaped her lips.

She was ready for more.

So was he.

Niko wanted to make her his wife in every sense of the word. He touched the thin straps on both sides of her nightgown, noticing her soft skin beneath the rough pads of his fingertips.

She pushed his hands away. "Not yet."

He didn't understand.

Before he could say anything, Isabel reached for a button on his shirt. "It's my turn."

As she worked with trembling hands to remove his shirt, Izzy's insides quivered with anticipation. Through the cotton, she felt the heat of his skin, the rise and fall of his chest. His breathing was no steadier than hers.

That made her feel better and quieted some of her

nerves.

Izzy hadn't done this before, but she'd overheard the guys at work. She knew what was supposed to happen. She wasn't about to let Niko do all the work tonight.

No way. No how.

She wanted him to enjoy their wedding night, too.

As she slid another button from its hole, her fingers shook.

"It's taking a long time," he said.

She moved on to the next button. "We're still on the warm-up lap."

"My tires are warm. I'm ready to race."

Izzy placed her palm over his heart. "Not yet."

His muscles rippled beneath the fabric. So athletic. So strong. He made her feel cherished. His.

It was all she could do not to sigh.

Was this how a wife was supposed to feel?

She wanted to be his, but she also wanted him to be hers.

Izzy's fingers fumbled on the last button. She brushed his shirt open, her hands grazing his warm skin. Tingles pulsed up her arms.

A key on a silver chain hung around his neck. The key to the bride box.

Izzy fingered it. "You're still wearing the key."

"Not anymore." He pulled the chain over his head and gave her the necklace. "The bride box is on the table next to the champagne. It belongs to you, my wife, once again."

She held the key. The box and its missing key had enabled Dee to force them together. But she didn't want to think about that tonight. "Thank you."

"You're welcome." His voice practically caressed. "Now toss the key on the floor so we can get back to what we were doing."

Izzy did.

Inching closer, she pushed the shirt over his broad shoulders and down his strong arms, arms that had carried her so effortlessly across the threshold as if she weighed nothing.

Her pulse skittered.

She wanted to memorize everything about him. His body showed the scars of war from his time as a soldier. Like the ribbons and medals he'd worn earlier, these were his badges of honor. He'd fought to protect Vernonia. She had no doubt he would fight to protect her.

A dizzying current of desire traveled through her.

Izzy traced the length of a scar running from his shoulder to his waist. She placed her palm over his ribs, her thumb rubbing another, smaller scar under his sternum.

He drew in a sharp breath.

She pulled her hand away. "Sorry."

"No, it's fine."

"I'm not sure what I'm supposed to do next."

"You don't have to worry about that." Niko raised

her hand to his mouth and kissed each of her fingers. "But you're overdressed."

He reached for the strap of her nightgown.

"The lights?"

With a swoop of his arms, Niko lifted her and then carried her toward the head of the bed. He set her on her feet so she was standing in front of him.

He pressed a button on the nightstand. The lights went off, but the candles around the room provided a romantic glow. "More comfortable now?"

Izzy nodded, feeling shy. She wasn't like the other women in his life, the polished, beautiful ones.

He pushed the straps of her nightgown off her shoulders.

Izzy's cheeks warmed.

Slowly his gaze raked over her. Appreciative. Seductive. Possessive.

Her heart jolted.

"You are stunning. Enchanting." His hands moved over her. Shivers of delight followed his touch. "Captivating."

Her insides melted. "Kiss me."

His lips captured hers again. This time with urgency and need. Izzy's heart sang. He needed her.

She returned his kisses with reckless abandon.

There was no turning back. She wanted him.

As they kissed, she gently touched him.

He inhaled sharply again. Captured her hand before easing her onto the mattress. Her head rested against a pillow.

The sound of his zipper brought a rush of emotions and an extra dose of nerves.

After removing his pants, he climbed onto the bed, the mattress dipping under his weight. As he lay over her, his hair fell forward, the long ends teasing her skin like a feather. The tantalizing scent of him surrounded her.

He lowered his head until his lips brushed hers.

Each touch, each kiss, sent shivers of pleasure radiating outward. He made her feel so desired, so sexy. She wanted to make him feel the same.

Boldly, Isabel touched him again. A low sound emerged from Niko's throat. She had no idea what she was doing, but his response gave her the courage to continue.

"We just started the race," Niko said. "But if you keep that up, I might have to black flag you."

His use of a racing term made her stomach tingle. "Why would you want to send me to the pits?"

Sweat dampened his forehead. "Breaking the rules."

"Forget the black flag. You can't penalize me for not knowing the rules." Her confidence spiraled because he enjoyed her touching him. "We have way too many laps to go to finish the race."

"Yellow then."

"Caution?"

He placed his hand over hers. "Slow down.

Otherwise you won't be able to avoid the debris on the track."

Laughing, she placed her hand on his chest. "Better."

A flash of humor crossed his face. "For you."

She showered kisses from his neck to his ear. "What's it going to take to get the green flag again?"

"Ready to race?"

She nodded enthusiastically. "You?"

"I think you can answer that question." He drew a line along her jawline. "I don't want to hurt you, but since it's your first time..."

If she had done this before, she would be more comfortable, confident. But despite her nerves, she was happy she'd waited until tonight.

Until him.

His heart beat beneath her palm. "I trust you."

Something flashed in his eyes. "I lapped you. Let's get you caught up."

Niko kissed her again until she thought her pounding heart might burst out of her chest. His lips and touch sent pulsations of pleasure radiating outward.

A fire ignited inside her, and she arched toward him. She wanted more, so much more.

Her heart swelled with happiness and something she'd never felt before. She pulled back. "Just so you know, the bride box is now mine and so are you."

Niko was the only man Izzy wanted. The only man

she would ever need. The only husband she could ever imagine having.

Chapter Seventeen

Lying in bed the next morning, Niko watched Isabel sleep. She curled against him, her legs wrapped around his. He needed to untangle himself so he could get out of bed, but he didn't want to wake her.

If Isabel woke, she would want to know where he was going. Niko had no idea. He only knew he wanted—needed—to get away. He enjoyed being with her, but he needed time to think.

He pulled one of his legs out from under hers.

Last night had been more than he could have hoped for or imagined. Isabel's curiosity and eagerness had surprised him and fueled his desire to make their wedding night perfect. He'd been powerless to resist her. She'd left him satisfied, spent, and wanting more.

So much more.

Wind blew into the room from an open balcony door.

He had been in such a hurry to get Isabel inside the room last night he had not thought to close the door. Privacy was an issue at the castle. He was usually more careful. But with Isabel, he lost all control. Case in point, the kiss during their wedding ceremony.

He shut the door.

Niko had taught himself to remain in control. He could count the times his temper had spiraled because he hated how not being in control felt. It reminded him of when Stefan had been killed, and Niko's world had been flipped upside down. He had lost so much, including his easier role in life as the spare heir. Nothing had taken away the pain and grief. Time had only dulled it. But he had known then he wanted to limit feeling that way again. That meant staying in control.

Last night, Niko had wanted to make Isabel his wife, but she had made him her husband. His body ached for her and his heart...

He raked his hand through his hair.

His heart needed to remain immune to her charms, her humor, her beauty, her seduction. Diving into the marriage *heart* first would not be smart because that would give her control over him.

He couldn't allow that to happen.

His priority was, and had to be, Vernonia. Nothing else could come first because so much needed to be done for his country to thrive, now and in the future. Distractions would get in the way. That included Isabel.

While falling in love with his wife made perfect sense on one hand, it didn't on the other because of Vernonia. He also wasn't ready to be in love. He didn't know when he would be ready.

Or if he ever would be.

He stared at his beautiful bride asleep in his bed.

This had nothing to do with her.

She had come willingly to him last night, but their marriage was the result of his father's underhanded tactics. There would be no divorce so there was no rush.

Niko would give her time to decide what she wanted from the marriage and from him. He might not be willing to give her his heart, but he would provide her with all that he could. He would do whatever was within his power to make their marriage successful.

He, however, would limit the distractions his marriage would bring. That meant not falling in love because that would be best for Vernonia.

And perhaps, himself.

Izzy didn't want to wake up. She was sore and tired, but she wanted to spend the rest of the day in bed with her husband.

Her husband.

As she remembered last night, heat flooded her face, making her cheeks burn. That didn't stop Izzy from reaching toward Niko. Her hand, however, found only space beside her.

She opened her eyes. He wasn't there. "Niko?"

No answer.

She hadn't expected to wake up alone. She wrapped herself in the sheet before checking the bathroom and the balcony. Not there, either.

A knock sounded.

Why would Niko knock to enter his own room? Izzy exchanged the sheet for her robe and opened the door. Mare stood with a tea cart containing breakfast. "Good morning, ma'am. The chef has prepared breakfast for you."

A breakfast for one based on the tray and silverware. A knot formed in her stomach. "Have you seen Prince Niko?"

"Yes, ma'am." Mare wheeled the cart into the room. "He's in his office."

Relief flooded Isabel. A thousand pounds seemed to lift from her shoulders. Before they left on their honeymoon, Niko must be trying to finish some work. Not surprising given his sense of responsibility. She admired that trait of his along with so many others.

Izzy enjoyed her meal on the balcony with the clear blue sky overhead and an occasional breeze. Hope replaced the dread she'd felt over her impending wedding day. Her entire outlook seemed to have shifted. The roses from the garden smelled fresher. The sun in the sky shone brighter. The smile on her face felt wider.

And her heart...

Eyes closed, she raised her face toward the sky. The sun's rays kissed Izzy's face. The heat against her skin reminded her of Niko. He cared about Vernonia with a fierce loyalty and love. She hoped he would come to care the same way about her. She dreamed of the day she could say *I love you* and hear him say that to her. Not as a careless whisper or a *quid pro quo*, but as the way he and his heart felt about her.

Her prince, her husband, her love.

Two hours later, Izzy stood in the drawing room with Boyd, Rowdy, and Duncan. The men had been enjoying their time in Vernonia.

Duncan handed her a business card. "I interviewed lawyers for you. I believe this one is the best suited to fairly represent your interests. He's from Sachestia."

Her birthland. She still found it difficult to believe that where a person was from still mattered in Vernonia. "Thank you. You've done so much for me."

"And your husband more than compensated me." Duncan hugged her. "Call me anytime. You're my most important princess client.”

“I’m your only princess client,” she replied.

Laughter filled his eyes. “Which makes you a VIP. Very important princess.”

Rowdy hugged her next. “You take care. Those royals mess with you, call. You’re family, and will always be one of us.”

A lump burned in her throat. She swallowed around it. “Thank you.”

Boyd stood in front of her. Concern clouded his normally carefree expression. “I’ll stay if that will make things easier for you, Iz.”

It would, but she couldn’t ask him to do that. He had his own life to live. She forced a smile when all she wanted to do was cling to her good friend. “You can’t stay. You have a brand-new truck waiting for you, courtesy of King Dmitar.”

Boyd shrugged. “My best friend’s more important than a truck.”

She blinked to keep the tears at bay. “Thanks, but I’ll be okay. Just promise you’ll come if I need you.”

“Say the word, and I’ll be on the next flight.”

Boyd hugged her. He didn’t seem to be in any hurry to let go. Neither was she. Finally, he loosened his arms and kissed her forehead. “Take care, Izzy.”

“You, too.”

As soon as the three left, Jovan whisked her outside.

Time to leave for the honeymoon, she assumed.

A few minutes later, Izzy walked beside Niko toward the helipad. Her nerve endings tingled as if she were about to be swept away for a magic carpet ride, only this one had a rotor and seats.

Niko said hello when she'd met him outside but nothing else. He was dressed casually in a polo shirt, khakis, and leather loafers. The man looked good no matter what he wore, but she preferred this style on him. He seemed more...real. The whole being royalty was still difficult for her.

"Where are we going?" she asked.

"You'll see soon enough." He sounded mysterious.

"I hope I packed the right clothes."

His brows furrowed. "I instructed Mare to pack for you."

Uh-oh. "I told her I'd do it myself."

"You must embrace your role as a princess of Vernonia, Isabel." Niko didn't sound upset, but he wasn't smiling.

Maybe she could fix that. "I'd rather embrace Vernonia's crown prince."

He didn't smile, but his eyes no longer appeared so serious. "You must embrace both."

He helped her into the helicopter, made sure her harness seat belt was on correctly, and then handed her a headset. "Wearing this will make communicating easier."

The takeoff went much faster than on her flight to Vernonia. The helicopter traveled north if her sense of direction was correct. A majestic mountain range with snowcapped peaks rose sharply into the sky. The contrast between the white and blue took her breath away.

The terrain, rugged and etched, reminded her of Niko. Warmth welled inside her. Her husband shared so many similarities with this land he loved. "It's beautiful."

"Yes." Staring out the window, he appeared preoccupied. Eager to make a connection like they'd shared last night, Izzy placed her hand on top of his.

He angled toward her though his smile didn't reach his eyes.

She wondered why he didn't lace his fingers with hers and hold her hand. After last night, she expected he would want to be closer to her. "Is something wrong?"

"No."

That didn't tell her anything. "Did you get your work completed?"

"Most of it, but that is not your concern."

Except it was when he was acting this way. Maybe something else was bothering him. "Tired?"

"I am fine," he said stiffly.

"You don't seem fine." She might not have experience with relationships, but his aloofness set off alarms in her head. "You're acting different."

His jaw thrust forward. "I am the same as I always am."

No, he wasn't. He'd been nicer, friendlier the day they met than he was right now. She pulled her hand away. He didn't seem to notice.

Hurt burrowed in deep. She crossed her arms over her chest.

Was the honeymoon over before it began?

Apprehensive, Izzy stared out the window. She didn't want to go into this vacation full of doubts and worry. Even though she was a good judge of people, she was still getting to know Niko. One night as husband and wife didn't enable her to read him like an open book.

Maybe nothing was wrong. Maybe he had work on his mind. For now, she would give him the benefit of the doubt. This marriage was new to him, too.

Pushing aside any troubling thoughts, she concentrated on the scenery. As pretty as a painting, villages dotted the landscape in the mountains and valley floor.

A castle appeared in the distance. Smaller than the one the royal family lived in, but just as fairy-tale-worthy with a tower and spires jutting into the sky.

She inhaled sharply.

As the helicopter flew closer, the castle was easier to see. A stone wall surrounded the grounds. Paths crisscrossed a carpet of lush green grass. Tall trees surrounded a crystal blue lake.

Wanting to see better, Izzy pressed her forehead against the window. "I love the castle."

"It's yours."

"Mine?"

"That is where you lived with your parents," he clarified. "It's your family home."

Her home? Izzy stared out the window in disbelief. "We're spending our honeymoon here?"

"Yes. Welcome to Sachestia. Not as warm as the beach."

"It's a million times better." Maybe she was overanalyzing Niko's words and actions. He'd put thought into where to spend their honeymoon. "It's perfect. Thanks."

The castle was even more spectacular in person, with more bedrooms than she could count, an obliging staff—many of whom were related to Uncle Frank— and a large six-bay garage that had the potential to be a mechanic's dream hangout.

She toured the castle's master suite, where they'd be staying. "This is the life."

"Better than Charlotte?" Niko asked.

"Different." She studied the ornate moldings and painted ceiling. "Have you spent much time here?"

"Not really," he admitted. "But my father stressed the importance of having it maintained for the people of Sachestia. So I have."

"You've done a lovely job."

"The staff deserves your praise. All I did was pay for it. Using your money," he joked.

"The funds were well spent." She moved closer to

him. "Can I thank the staff via proxy? You."

He eyed her with interest. "What did you have in mind?"

Izzy rose and placed her mouth against Niko's. As her lips moved over his, he tasted warm and a little salty. She loved the combination of flavors but drew away after a minute.

"I shall keep that thank-you to myself." Desire filled his eyes. "You can find a different way to express your gratitude to the staff."

"Okay, but…" Being with Niko made her bolder than she'd ever been. "I'm not finished with you."

This time, his smile not only reached his eyes but also crinkled the corners. "I shall lock the door so we are not disturbed while you...thank me."

Okay, she was right to let go of her worries about Niko in the helicopter. Whatever had been wrong seemed better, and she couldn't be more pleased. This was going to be the best honeymoon ever.

Chapter Eighteen

The honeymoon was going better than Niko had expected. His mornings consisted of work in an office he'd commandeered while Isabel slept in. He spent his days sightseeing with her, accompanied by security and staff that kept them from getting too close. And his nights...

A sense of contentment flowed through him.

Those were the best parts.

If Niko had his choice, he and Isabel would remain in the bedroom until it was time to go home. But as appealing as that option was, he needed Isabel to see where her family was from, and they needed to be seen by the people who lived in the northern part of Vernonia. Besides, he could not allow himself to fall for his beautiful wife.

That would be a…mistake.

"Good morning." She descended the stairs. Her faded jeans fit like a second skin. Her lavender short-sleeved shirt complemented her coloring. "I was told to dress casually."

"What you have on is perfect."

Her face lit up, and his pulse stuttered. He would have to work on not allowing that to happen.

She joined him in the foyer. "Where are we going today?"

"You shall see." He held up his hand to stop her from asking more. "Boyd mentioned you enjoyed surprises so I will not be providing you more information."

"I do enjoy surprises. At least, good ones."

Niko's jaw tensed. He hated thinking about the bad ones she must have faced and how she and Franko must have struggled in Charlotte. Her life would be better in Vernonia. Niko would see to that.

A guard opened the front doors.

Niko motioned for her to go first. "You will enjoy this one."

"I am intrigued."

He was, too. With her. A bit too much. "Patience, Highness."

"I shall try, Highness."

After two hours of hiking, they neared their destination. Niko motioned to the guards who were following them to remain where they were. This was one surprise he wanted to share with Isabel alone.

Niko laced his fingers with hers. Her skin wasn't soft, but it was warm. Her hand was strong and fit perfectly with his.

"We're almost there." He squeezed. "Close your eyes."

"And then I'll see my surprise?"

He nodded. "We have a short distance to go."

Her eyelids closed. "Lead the way, Highness. I'm at your mercy."

If he weren't careful, he would be at hers.

Knowing she trusted him without hesitation sent his heart galloping like the wild horses roaming the lower foothills.

With careful steps, he led her to the lookout point and stopped. The clear sky provided views of Sachestia all the way to the horizon. Niko had been following the weather forecast to assure a beautiful day.

"You can open your eyes now."

Isabel did. She gasped. Squeezed his hand. "This is... So beautiful..."

Her voice was soft but filled with the same awe as was written on her face.

She was the beautiful one.

Staring at the view, she leaned into him. "I love my

surprise. I... Thank you, Niko."

The affection in her voice sent joy shooting through him. He wrapped his arm around Isabel, pulling her close. Her vanilla and jasmine scent surrounded him.

He was supposed to be keeping his distance when they were out and about, but this one time wouldn't hurt anything. He brushed his lips over her hair.

For now, he and Isabel could be husband and wife, newlyweds on their honeymoon, enjoying this time together and each other. Their real life and their royal duties would intrude soon enough, but a part of Niko wished they could stay like this...forever.

The days passed in a blur for Izzy. As she dressed one morning, she wondered what was on today's agenda. So far, she and Niko explored the castle's land, toured the nearby quaint, mountain villages, and visited with the friendly people who wanted to welcome the royal newlyweds. More than once, he'd invited others on their excursions or for meals. Sometimes both. She didn't know if having others around, even on their honeymoon, was part of being a royal. Maybe Niko wanted to be more inclusive during his time in Sachestia given the turbulent past.

But she'd finally gotten her wish—time alone with

Niko without having to be in their bedroom. They strolled the palace grounds. No guards or staff or guests had been invited along. A giddiness filled Izzy.

"Sachestia is so lovely." She strayed toward the edge of the path where flowers grew and their fragrance scented the air. A lovely yellow blossom caught her eye. "Wherever I look, I see something more breathtaking than what I saw last."

He slowed his pace until she caught up to him. "Like yesterday."

Nodding, she remembered how standing at the top of Mount Rajin with him had made her feel so cherished and special. That the future was full of so much possibility.

"Are you enjoying yourself?" she asked.

"Very much." He glanced at a squirrel. "Sachestia is special."

A sigh welled inside her. "I want to learn as much as I can about it."

"You have a castle library full of books, a staff eager to answer your questions, and people who would love to share their stories and past."

"I must take advantage of those things before we leave." She glanced his way. "Or come back?"

"That is always an option."

"Good." She moved closer to Niko.

Had her mother and father walked these same paths? Kissed with the gorgeous views as backdrops? Fallen in love while exploring this charming yet rugged mountainous land?

That could happen to her and Niko.

Izzy wanted to hold his hand, but his arms swung out of reach as he walked.

Not the first time.

Which told her they needed to bring the deeper connection they experienced in the bedroom to other places.

She wanted to give him her mind and soul, not just her body.

During those precious moments together in bed, he gave her a taste of the intimacy she yearned for—a glimpse of how wonderful all parts of their marriage could be, not only the physical side. The time whetted her desire for an unbreakable emotional bond because her love for him kept growing despite things not being perfect between them. But she hated how once they left the bedroom, the closeness they'd forged vanished as if an invisible wall had been erected between them.

He'd admitted not having experience with relationships, so maybe the issue was two people unsure how to proceed with each other and needing to learn how to do that.

"You have a thoughtful expression on your face." He studied her. "What's on your mind?"

Did she dare? She had nothing to lose. "How I wish you were holding my hand."

He shortened his stride and held her hand but didn't lace his fingers with hers. "All you have to do is ask."

"I will the next time." She only wished she wouldn't have to ask, that holding hands and wanting to touch was something he wanted, too. "And you can do the same."

She hoped with her whole heart he would.

A bird took flight from a tree.

Smiling, Izzy watched it soar higher into the blue sky. She wasn't a cartoon princess with animal friends who spoke to her and helped her clean, but she was hopeful a happy ending, one usually reserved for storybooks and movies, awaited her and Niko.

Emotion swelled. "I love this castle. The people. The villages."

You.

Izzy wanted so much more from their marriage. She wanted to lose herself and her heart in Niko. Patience. She needed to not push too hard, but holding back wasn't easy for her.

"You're happy here," he said.

"Being here..." *With you.* "It feels like..."

He stopped and faced her. "What?"

"Home."

Niko studied her, his gaze warm and affectionate, but in a flash, that disappeared, replaced by an unfriendly expression.

"That is because Sachestia *is* your home." Niko's matter-of-fact tone bristled. "You can return whenever you wish."

You, not we.

It was only one word, but combined with the other signs was enough.

Was patience going to be enough? She'd thought so only a minute ago, but now...

Disappointment squeezed her heart.

Izzy hadn't believed Niko would fall in love with her on their honeymoon, but she'd been hopeful it would happen. Someday.

But for now...

The hope of love blossoming withered. The promise of "until death do us part" became a dull ache in her chest. The possibility of a happily ever after faded.

Izzy might want more with her husband, but he didn't appear to want the same with her. She had no idea what that would mean long-term. Would physical intimacy be all Niko offered? If so, would that be enough for her?

Did she have a choice if it wasn't?

A few days later, Niko rowed Isabel across the lake in a small boat. All her enthusiasm and energy from their nights together disappeared in the light of day. He did not know what had caused the change in her, but she seemed to have shut down, only answering when spoken to and not wanting to leave the castle.

He studied her. "You are tired."

"I'm...not."

Niko waited for her to say more. She did not.

That must be his fault. His trying to distance himself from her was finally working. At first, she would not let him push her away, but lately she no longer seemed to care if they talked or remained silent. Even things in the bedroom where everything had been perfect, was different.

She was different.

"You are not talkative today."

Isabel shrugged. "We don't have much time left here."

A pair of birds flew over the water. A frog croaked. The smell of freshly mowed grass from the lush lawns bordering the lake hung in the air, but he would rather inhale her scent.

Niko wanted...what he could not have. "It is too bad we cannot stay longer."

She perked up. "Really?"

"Yes." He enjoyed spending time with her even if things were tense at times. "I have not relaxed this much since... I cannot remember when."

Her shoulders sagged again. "Me either."

He hated seeing her this way. "You do not appear relaxed."

"I'm worried what happens after we leave."

Niko could kiss away her worry, but he wanted to

be honest with her. "Things will be different when we go home."

She trailed the tips of her fingers in the water, leaving a small wake behind them. "How so?"

"Once we are at the main castle, we will not be spending as much time together as here." Unexpected relief crossed her features. Niko did not understand nor like it. "You will be expected to assume your role as a princess of Vernonia."

"Right away?" The words flew out.

Perhaps if Isabel had something more to do, she would be happier. "How does tomorrow sound? Regional officials have requested our presence at a village celebration. This will be the perfect introduction to your new duties."

She shook her head. "We're on our honeymoon."

"Yes, but they only want us to take part in the parade. It should not take long."

Isabel bit her lip. "I'm not sure I'm ready for that."

"All you have to do is smile and wave." Not much could go wrong with the outing. "The parade will be an excellent way for those who remember your parents to see you as their princess."

She wrung her hands. "What if I fall on my face?"

"You will be sitting in a carriage."

Isabel stuck out her tongue at him.

He grinned, relieved her playfulness had returned. "If you fall, I will catch you."

An unreadable expression formed on her face. Her

eyes had lost their twinkle. "I guess it would be okay."

He had hoped for more enthusiasm, but at least she was willing to take her place as a Vernonian princess. That pleased him. "Thank you, Isabel."

Her gaze darkened. "Is this what my life will be like? Parades and whatnot?"

"You shall be expected to make public appearances, go on outings, attend openings. You will get used to the routine."

The corners of her mouth turned down. "Sounds like a lot of fluff. Princess waving and cutting ribbons."

Her tone made the tasks sound so trivial. "Some fluff is involved, but people expect the royal family to participate in events. It is an important part of our duties."

"Duty or not, I'm not a fluff person." Her lower lip thrust forward. "I prefer to do tasks. Help people. Accomplish something I can see or touch. That's one reason I enjoy being a mechanic."

"What is another reason?"

"Cars are awesome." She splashed him. "Which you would know if you ever drove instead of being chauffeured."

Niko splashed her back. He had missed this side of their relationship. If they kept things less serious and emotional, they could have more fun. "You will accomplish many things and help people with your solo agenda."

Her arms dropped to her sides. "My what?"

"Good Works," he clarified. "The social issues, charities, and causes you will focus your energies on apart from the ones we work on together."

"Are these Good Works one of my duties?" she asked.

He nodded. "The entire country will follow what you choose."

As the twinkle returned to her eyes, the knot in his stomach loosened. "I know the best Good Works ever."

Her excitement appealed to him at a gut level. "What is that?"

"I could bring a Formula One race to Vernonia."

Of course she would focus on cars and racing. Niko dug the oars into the water to take a deeper stroke. He needed to steer her away from that idea. "Grand Prix is an interesting thought, but I am confident you will think of something else."

"Think about it. Please." Two little lines formed above her nose. "A race sponsored by a long-lost American princess would provide Vernonia with good press and tourist dollars."

"Most princesses focus on education or health issues. That is why they are called Good Works."

She slid him a furtive glance. "I'm not like other princesses."

"But you are working on that, right?" he half teased.

Her shoulders slumped. "Cars and racing are my

things. Why can't I combine those with a Good Work?"

"Having your own interests is fine, but you are Her Royal Highness Crown Princess Isabel of Vernonia," Niko explained. "You will become a role model."

Isabel frowned, her eyebrows knotting. "You don't think I can be a role model as I am."

It was not a question. She sounded annoyed and a little sad, something happening more often with each passing day.

"If you make your contemporary outlook more appealing to the masses, you will be a stronger role model."

Isabel crossed her arms over her chest. "So I'm not appealing, either."

"That is not what I meant."

"What *do* you mean?" Her voice rose and not in a good way. "You talk about wanting to modernize Vernonia yet you cling to outdated stereotypes. You should show Vernonians that views are changing."

"Show, yes, but we cannot shock people into progress."

"My working as a mechanic is not shocking. Neither is bringing an F-one race to Vernonia. It's an excellent idea. One you shouldn't dismiss without at least considering it."

"Change takes time." Izzy had a stubborn side. Niko did not want her to dig in her heels about this. "Before you become too attached to this race idea, consider what Julianna might do."

Isabel winced. "You want me to be like Jules?"

"She would be an excellent role model to emulate when choosing Good Works."

Isabel's jaw tightened. "I don't know what Jules might choose, but I know something she wouldn't do."

"What?"

Isabel grabbed an oar and threw it into the water on the starboard side of the rowboat.

Forget stubborn. She was being ungracious.

Niko reached for the oar. "You are not being nice."

Isabel stood. "I'm only getting started."

He did not know what she had in mind, but he had never heard the edge in her voice. "Sit down before you fall overboard."

She leaned over toward one side.

"Isa—"

The boat tipped.

Niko splashed into the cold water. Isabel, too.

He reached for her so he could help her into the rowboat, but she dodged his arm.

"Come here," he shouted.

She lay on her back, floating and kicking to put distance between them. "Jules is my friend, but I don't want to be like her. I'm not a lump of clay to be molded into the perfect princess. I want to be me. You should want that, too."

Isabel flipped over and swam toward the shore. Each long, graceful stroke took her farther away from him. The security detail on shore scrambled into the water.

Niko gathered the oars, climbed into the rowboat, and watched her with a sinking feeling in his gut.

The honeymoon was not scheduled to end for two more days, but it was over now.

Niko rowed to shore. He had no idea what this meant for him and Isabel long-term. He was not sure he wanted to know.

Chapter Nineteen

The next day, an overcast sky hid the afternoon sun. Emil, the castle butler and Uncle Frank's cousin, predicted rain would fall on the parade. The weather wasn't ideal for the village's celebration, but the gray matched Izzy's mood perfectly.

She hadn't spoken to Niko since the incident on the lake. He'd eaten dinner elsewhere and slept in another room last night. He'd skipped breakfast, so she hadn't seen him this morning.

All she wanted to do was crawl deeper under the covers and cry, but that wasn't what a princess did. At least according to Jules, who Izzy had called asking for advice. Hoping for the best seemed the only option. That really sucked.

During the drive to the village, an icy silence consumed the limousine's interior. Izzy didn't know what to say to Niko. If she'd argued with a guy she dated, she never went out with him again. Fighting seemed like a waste of time and energy. But that meant she'd never learned how to deal with conflict. Niko was remaining quiet so she would follow his lead.

After they arrived, she took a seat in the charming horse-drawn carriage decorated with fresh, colorful wildflowers.

Niko sat next to her. "Ready?"

The space between them on the bench seat felt as wide as the infield at the Indy 500. She forced a smile for the villagers' benefit. "No, but I think it's too late for them to cancel the parade. Unless Emil is right about a rainstorm."

"The people would be disappointed," Niko said flatly.

Villagers lined the narrow street, waving every imaginable size of Vernonian flags. "It reminds me of the Fourth of July parades back home except nothing is red, white, and blue."

"Each of the colors in the Vernonian flag has a special meaning. The light blue represents the sky, that our country may be as tranquil as the heavens above. The white stands for purity of heart and action. The yellow crest is the color of the sun as it faithfully rises each day we pledge our loyalty to remain faithful to one another."

"That's so meaningful and lovely." She had much to learn about this land and its history. "I don't know whether the story behind the colors of the U.S. flag is fact or fiction."

"If this were the Fourth of July, you would be eating hot dogs and hamburgers."

"Yeah." She motioned to her designer skirt, cropped jacket, hat, gloves, and high heels. "Though I would never be dressed like this. I'd be wearing jeans or shorts and a T-shirt."

"People came to see a princess today."

A Sachestian princess. The future queen. Anxiety fluttered. "I know."

She didn't want to disappoint them, which was why she'd worn the clothing the maid had laid out this morning. But even though Izzy wore a fancy outfit and answered to Her Royal Highness or ma'am, she was the same inside as she'd always been. Nothing would change that.

Not a new wardrobe.

Not princess lessons.

Not a prince for a husband.

If only Niko could accept her as she was, their marriage might stand a chance. As it was...

Izzy adjusted her white gloves and focused on the people. The friendly waves from the villagers lessened her apprehension.

In front of their carriage, a pickup truck pulled a float carrying folk dancers dressed in traditional costumes. A marching band played behind them. The boom of a bass drum matched the beat of her heart, a combination of the anxiety over the parade and her marriage.

She waved and smiled, as did Niko, but he remained silent. The villagers didn't seem to notice the strain between them. For that, Izzy was thankful.

The carriage jerked to a stop. The driver set the brake. The two horses whinnied and pawed at the ground.

The float in front of them had stopped, too.

A local official rushed up to the carriage.

"What is happening?" Niko asked him.

"The truck pulling the dancers' float has broken down, Your Royal Highness. We are summoning a mechanic."

Finally, a chance to be useful. Izzy hopped out of the carriage with no assistance from the security.

Niko followed her. "What are you doing?"

She straightened her skirt. "They need a mechanic."

"You are a princess."

"Why can't I be both?" Izzy kept her voice low and a smile on her face. Jules would be so proud.

"It's inappropriate," Niko said under his breath. "Unacceptable."

She removed her white gloves. "The parade must go on."

"Don't do this, Isabel. The people—"

"I am more like these people than you."

"No, you are not. Do not think otherwise. There will be consequences."

"You're overreacting." Izzy thought about Diana, the Princess of Wales. She'd been known as the People's Princess. She hadn't been given that title by sitting around and waiting for others to take charge. And the two women—both commoners—who had married princes in the United Kingdom. They were helping to modernize the monarchy in a positive way. "I know what I'm doing."

He pressed his lips together.

Annoyance flared. "Please stop with that royal stiff-upper-lip thing you do."

"I don't know what you're talking about."

As Izzy hurried past the float with the dancers, she tucked her gloves into a jacket pocket.

An official fell into step with her. "How may I help, Your Royal Highness?"

"I'm going to see if I can fix the truck."

The man gasped. "We need a mechanic, ma'am."

Izzy raised her chin. "I am a mechanic."

And a good one.

The truck's hood was propped open. Several people stood there contemplating the inner workings of the vehicle.

"The engine didn't die." The truck driver scratched his balding head. "But the truck won't move."

Izzy nudged her way through several festively clad dancers. "Excuse me."

The group parted for her like the Red Sea. The scent of motor oil from the engine smelled better than perfume, but the truck had to be older than her. She kicked off her heels and climbed on the grill to peer inside. It had a carburetor. She checked the hoses and the fan belt. Grease dirtied her hands. One of her fingernails chipped. For the truck to stop moving, something must have broken or come undone. And that was when she saw the problem. "A-ha. A broken throttle linkage to the carburetor."

Izzy sensed rather than felt Niko move right behind her.

"Let someone else fix it," he whispered.

"I know how to do it." She noticed those standing around weren't smiling. "I need a pair of glasses. Sunglasses would work, too. Wire-rimmed ones would probably be easiest. I promise to replace them."

An official stepped forward with an expression of disdain, but he handed her his glasses.

"Thank you." Izzy broke off an earpiece. She threaded it through the linkage and twisted the ends together. She lowered the hood and stepped out of the way. "That should do it."

The truck driver shifted into gear. The truck rolled forward. "It worked."

The crowd was quiet—dead silent. People stared with shock and disappointment on their faces.

She didn't understand. The parade could continue, but the only ones smiling at her were the children and teenagers. They flashed her the thumbs-up sign. A few clapped. The littlest ones jumped up and down.

There will be consequences.

An old man shook his head. Two men frowned. A group of women whispered and motioned to her.

Izzy hurried to the carriage and climbed aboard. She brushed her dirty hands together, wishing for a wet wipe. Grease stained her skirt.

A crisp white handkerchief appeared at the end of Niko's extended arm. His tight jaw and narrowed lips told her he wasn't happy. He could join the club.

Izzy took it and wiped her hands. "I don't see why everyone is so upset."

The carriage lurched forward.

"People came expecting to see a princess. Someone special, not like themselves." Niko snatched the handkerchief from her and wiped her chin. "Instead, they see a woman who doesn't care enough to keep her clothes clean for them. Or herself. Your hands are dirty. Your fingernails are now chipped. They feel cheated and disrespected."

Heat burned her cheeks. So much judgment. Not only from Niko but also those in the crowd. "I wanted to win the people over by helping."

"You could have accomplished that by walking out

to the crowd and visiting with them while the truck was repaired. You could have told someone what to fix instead of insisting you do it yourself."

Humiliation flowed through her veins. She put on gloves over her dirty hands. "You never told me."

"You never gave me a chance, but can you honestly say you would have listened?"

A young mother held onto a toddler. Smiling, she waved at Izzy.

"Not everyone is disappointed," she countered. His anger matched her own. "The older generation is, but those who are younger and the children seem ready to embrace change."

"We have a duty to *all* Vernonians." His harsh voice sliced into her like a blade. "We cannot ignore the older people in favor of those who are young."

Izzy stiffened, but she continued to wave and smile at the villagers along the parade route. Several teenagers greeted her with cheers, but the older people remained silent, a sign of their disapproval.

"This is who I am," she said quietly.

"You are not a commoner, Isabel." Niko waved at a small girl holding a green balloon. "You are the special woman willing to sacrifice your future and your dreams for your country. You are Royal Highness Crown Princess Isabel of Vernonia. It's time you acted like her."

As she blew a kiss to a little boy sitting on his father's shoulders and holding a small American flag,

Niko's words sank in.

A horrible realization washed over her. "You will never accept Izzy Poussard, mechanic and race car fanatic."

His jaw jutted forward. "It is time for you to leave the past behind and move on."

"The way you want Vernonia to move on without changing your outdated views?"

"I told you change takes time. I know what Vernonia needs."

My father believes Vernonia needs an heir. He wants one as soon as possible.

Izzy's heart dropped. Her worst fear was turning out to be true. Niko hadn't wanted to go on a honeymoon to start their marriage off right. He'd wanted her to get pregnant. That was why things were so great between them in the bedroom but not anywhere else.

Her breathing hitched.

Their marriage had been a sham from the beginning. Love wasn't a possibility.

"You don't want a wife. The only thing you want is a baby." Her insides twisted. "You said you'd be honest with me, but you haven't been. You're no different from your father."

The ride from the village to the castle was frigid. The

silence seemed to push Isabel further away from Niko. He longed to reach out to her, but he couldn't. Not when he was so on edge and ready to snap.

He'd been at war, caught in firefights and attacked, but he'd never faced a situation like this. Anger, frustration, hurt, and something unfamiliar he couldn't define swirled inside him. He needed to keep the emotions in check so he wouldn't lose control. That would only make matters worse.

The limousine stopped in front of the castle. Isabel slid from the car and marched inside like a soldier on a mission.

Niko followed her upstairs and into their bedroom. He closed the door so they wouldn't be disturbed or overheard.

She took a deep breath. "This was a big mistake."

Relief nearly knocked him over. Isabel understood she had let him down—had let herself down. That explained her outburst. "Send a formal apology to the village. Tell them you apologize for your lapse in judgment and inappropriate behavior during the parade. Everything will be fine."

Her mouth gaped. "I'm not talking about the parade. I'm talking about our marriage."

Anger surged. The emotion he'd been holding in exploded like a volcano. "You mean the marriage I was trapped into?"

A stunned expression formed on her face before her features hardened in a way he hadn't seen before.

Not even on the rowboat. Her hands balled into fists.

"It's not as if *I* wanted to marry *you!*" Her eyes glistened, but no tears fell. She raised her chin, lines forming above the bridge of her nose. "I want to be in an equal partnership with a man who will accept me, love me for who I am, not for who he wants me to be."

Pushing her shoulders back, she straightened. "I want to be a wife, not a duty or obligation that has to be juggled with other responsibilities."

Izzy stared down the length of her nose. "I don't want to be married to a man who keeps me at arm's length and only wants to have sex with me because he needs an heir and a spare for his marriage to be deemed successful."

Each emotionally charged word pummeled into him like a fist. The uproar in his head made thinking impossible. Niko had married her. Again. He resented her for wanting more from him.

He took a breath. And another. His blood pressure continued spiraling. "We've only known each other a few weeks. This was never supposed to be a starry-eyed romance or a love match."

Her mouth twisted. "You've made it clear that's not what you want from me and our marriage."

"Would you rather I lie and tell you what you want to hear?"

"I want you to be honest, Niko."

"I have been honest!" His voice sounded harsh, raw. He didn't know how to handle the rush of emotions. "I've tried to be honest with you since we met."

"No, you led me to believe we might have more than a state marriage, but that's not true, is it?"

He swallowed. "A state marriage is for the best."

The pain flashing across her face nearly undid him. She straightened.

"Now it's my turn to be honest." Her gaze bored into him. "I'm not sure I can do a state marriage the way I thought I could. I don't get this whole royal duty thing. I'm not sure I ever will."

His heart skipped a beat. "Isabel—"

She held up her hand, and he stopped talking.

"I will never be the perfect princess you want for Vernonia. I'll never be like Jules." Isabel's voice cracked. "I won't be a royal broodmare, either. I need time to think, to figure out what I want to do."

His lungs constricted. He struggled to breathe. "Do?"

"Whether I remain in Vernonia or go home to Charlotte."

Her words stunned him. She must be hurting to consider returning to the U.S. after agreeing to stay. "Isabel—"

"I don't want to cause another conflict, but from what I saw today, the older generation is the problem. I have to believe the younger generation, the ones who would be asked to go to war, would stand up for what is right and refuse to fight."

"We agreed to figure this out together."

"The only place we're together is in bed. Sex won't solve the problems between us." The pain on her face was undeniable, and knowing he was the direct cause hurt. "I need to figure things out on my own."

"No."

She raised her chin. "It's time for you to go."

Unfamiliar panic flared. He didn't want to leave her. Lose her. "Please don't do this."

"You've left me no choice."

Feelings overwhelmed him, conquered his tentative control. In a swift move, he pulled her to him and crushed his lips against hers in a brutal kiss. Isabel didn't back away but returned his kiss.

He didn't know how to express what he was feeling, didn't understand the war of emotions, but he could show her. Niko poured his feelings into the kiss until she clung to him.

Finally, regretfully, he drew back. The same passion, the same confusion he felt reflected in her eyes. "I shall leave you now."

Chapter Twenty

Several weeks passed. Izzy remained at her family's castle. The only contact with Niko had been a month ago when a package of documents arrived transferring her father's estate, including ownership of the castle, to her. He hadn't emailed, texted, or called her.

Maybe that was why she'd felt so tired and crummy lately.

A broken heart?

She hoped not.

Izzy hadn't figured out what she should do or

where she should go. She couldn't stop thinking about the way Niko had kissed her before he left. His desperation had been real, palpable, but if that was the case, if he had feelings for her, why hadn't he been in touch?

There was one person she could call who might be able to help...

"You're hurting. I can hear it in your voice," Jules said after Izzy explained what had happened. "But this might be for the best."

Izzy hadn't expected her friend to say that. "Me returning to Charlotte?"

"No, Izzy. Charlotte is the last place you should go." Compassion and understanding filled Jules's voice. "You need time to figure out who you are and who you want to be."

"I'm Izzy Poussard."

"Yes, but you're also Princess Isabel, wife of the crown prince and the only member of the Sachestian royal family."

"This country is whacked."

Jules laughed. "Not as much as Aliestle."

"They're both backward."

"True, and you're the perfect person to bring the modern woman to Vernonia's old-fashioned ways of thinking. Change must happen, but a balance is required, and you're the only one who can determine what that might be."

Izzy shook her head. "I'm not like you."

"That's a good thing. A benefit in your favor." Jules once again surprised Izzy. "The system needs to be challenged. I wish I could do that, but any sign of rebellion would destroy my family and everything I've been raised to do. But you, Izzy Poussard Kresimir, can, in a gentle, respectful way that will have a lasting effect for all of Vernonia."

Izzy felt nauseous. She clutched her stomach with her free hand. "How can I do that? I'm just a mechanic from Charlotte."

"Oh, Izzy, you are so much more than that. You are a princess. You always have been. It's time you believed it. Not only in your mind but also in your heart."

When Izzy hung up, she was no closer to deciding what to do. Or close to believing what Jules had said. Still, Izzy remained in Sachestia to learn more about her father's family. She spent her days visiting the various villages in the area, meeting the people, and working the land as a harvest came around. Not exactly princess behavior, but slowly she made inroads with the villagers after the parade fiasco.

The older generation seemed to have fixed ideas like Niko about what royalty should do and whom they should be, but those who were younger didn't, especially the teenagers and children. They accepted Izzy as she was. Some wanted to know more about cars, so she offered to teach them about basic car repairs. Fifteen children showed up. The village official had told her to expect five.

During the class, she bent over.

The room spun. She grabbed hold of the table holding her tools.

"Princess, are you okay?" a young girl asked.

"I'm fine." Izzy didn't feel great, but she didn't want to worry anyone. "A little light-headed."

An older boy rolled a chair across the floor. "Please sit, ma'am."

Izzy did.

"My father is a doctor." A girl around ten studied Izzy. "We should take you to see him."

The others agreed and rolled her in the chair to a small medical clinic in the village.

The doctor was in his mid-forties, nice, and thorough with the tests he ran. She sat in the exam room alone waiting for the results.

"I have good news, ma'am," he said on his return.

"I'm healthy?"

"Yes, and you're also pregnant."

Pregnant. With Niko's child.

She sat frozen, too stunned to feel anything.

"How...?" She'd been so overwhelmed and stressed that she hadn't thought about her period. It had never been regular before, but still... "I mean, I know how, but how far along?"

"I want to do an ultrasound so we can figure that out."

Izzy nodded, unable to speak. She could narrow

down the dates to the week, the only week they'd spent together as husband and wife. That would make her seven, possibly eight weeks pregnant.

The royal broodmare had fulfilled her duty without trying. Izzy didn't know whether to laugh or cry.

A baby.

A surge of love, strong and protective, flowed through her. She hugged her stomach. If only Niko were...

But he wasn't.

Would you rather I lie and tell you what you want to hear?

No, but Izzy's heart splintered. The baby she carried was as much his as hers. Keeping the news from him would be cruel and unforgivable.

As soon as the ultrasound was completed, she would call him. Even if he were the last person she wanted to talk to.

Niko sat behind his desk in his office. The computer screen blurred. He rubbed his eyes.

The long hours were catching up with him. But only work filled the void these past weeks.

Not *void*.

The space next to him in bed. In the garden. At the dining room table. Wherever he was.

But work could not touch the space in his heart.

Nothing could. Or would.

Except Isabel.

She had wanted to figure things out on her own so he was giving her the time and distance she desired. He assumed she would call when she was ready to see him, but so far she had not. He hated every minute—each second—they were apart.

He had gone to the garage every day. Being there made him feel closer to her even if that was all in his mind.

Niko's forehead throbbed. He massaged his temples to stave off another headache.

In the outer office where Jovan worked, a phone rang.

Niko stretched the cords of muscles in his neck. When he finished, he saw his aide standing in front of his desk.

"There is a call for you, sir," Jovan said.

"You deal with it."

"It's Princess Isa—"

Niko grabbed the receiver off his desk. "Isabel."

His aide headed out of the office and closed the door.

"Hey, Niko."

Hearing her voice for the first time in seven weeks filled him with an odd mixture of relief and regret. "You received the estate transfer paperwork."

"Yes, thank you. My attorney said everything was in perfect order."

"Good."

Except it was not. This situation was horrible, but he had no idea how to fix things between them. His feelings were a mishmash of emotions he did not understand, but one thing was certain—he missed her.

Uncomfortable silence filled the line.

He had always known what to say, but Isabel left him as tongue-tied as a schoolboy with his first crush. Except she was his wife. She needed to be with him. "I—"

"I didn't call about the papers," she said at the same time.

"Excuse me," he said. "Tell me why you phoned."

She took a breath and then exhaled. "I—I'm pregnant."

He gripped the phone. "You are what?"

"Pregnant."

He absorbed the word, letting it flow through him. The news would send his parents rejoicing. His country, too.

"There's more," she added.

"More?" he repeated.

"I'm pregnant with twins."

His mouth gaped. He closed it. "Twins."

"Yes. An heir and a spare in one shot."

He would have laughed except for the serious edge to her tone and the hidden meaning behind her words.

"I hope you are happy." Her voice was devoid of any emotion.

"I am thrilled." The pregnancy would get them back on track. They could work out their issues and be together again. "I will be there tomorrow to bring you home."

"This doesn't change anything."

His muscles tensed. "But you are pregnant."

"Pregnant, Niko, not sick." She sounded annoyed. "At least not yet. The doctor warned me morning sickness could happen."

No. This would not do. "You need to be examined by a physician at the university hospital."

"I'm satisfied and happy with the village doctor."

"But—"

"I'm staying here." Her tone held a note of finality. "I thought you should know about the babies."

His temper spiraled, but he needed to remain calm. For his sake. For hers. And the babies. Upsetting Isabel again would only make matters worse.

She was in Sachestia, not the United States. For that, he was grateful. But if he said the wrong thing, he could send her away for good. He could not allow that to happen.

He wanted to say so many things, but settled on something that would not escalate things between them. "Thank you."

"I'd rather the news remain within the family and close members of the staff until after the first trimester, in case I miscarry. You never know what might happen this early and since it's my first pregnancy."

His chest ached from being apart when she was going through this on her own. "Is the doctor concerned?"

"No, but I'd rather not have to deal with a loss publicly."

Niko knew nothing about pregnancy so he would need a crash course. He scribbled a note to Jovan to buy books. "I understand."

"Thanks." She cleared her throat. Perhaps she wasn't so unaffected by all this as she sounded. "My next appointment is in two weeks if you want to come with me."

"Yes," Niko said without hesitation, thankful for the invitation. "I will clear my calendar."

But two weeks?

That was fourteen days away.

He did not want to wait that long to see her.

"I'll send the information to Jovan," she added.

To Jovan.

Niko's insides twisted. He hated this wall between them. "Fine, but would you mind if I visited you? Before the appointment? Say, this weekend."

The silence might as well have been a death knell for their marriage. His fingernails dug into his palm on his free hand. If he squeezed the phone any harder it might break.

"I can stay somewhere else, if that would make you more comfortable," he added.

Just please let me see you. If only for a few minutes.

He needed to check on her, to make certain she was okay. Healthy. Happy. That was what a husband and father should do, right?

"You can visit if you want." She sounded hesitant, but she hadn't said no. "The castle has plenty of rooms, so you can stay here."

But not with me.

The words were unspoken but implied.

Niko would not complain. He would make the most of the opportunity. "Thank you. I look forward to our visit."

"Okay, then."

No. He was not ready to let her go. "If you need anything…"

"Goodbye, Niko. See you when you arrive."

She hung up before he could reply.

Emotion roiling through him, Niko rose from his desk, exited his office, and made the familiar walk to the king's office.

His father's assistant looked up from his computer monitor. "The king—"

"Will see me now." Niko pushed past the royal guards, opened the door himself, and entered his father's office.

His father hung up the phone. "Niko—"

"Isabel is pregnant with twins."

"Even better than I hoped for. I'm sorry for manipulating you and Izzy, but I knew in my heart she was what we needed—not only as a member of the royal family, but as one of *our* family. It's clear the two of you belong together." A wide grin lit up his father's face. "When does she arrive home?"

"She is staying in Sachestia. She is still trying to figure things out."

"Have you figured out anything during your...separation?" his father asked as if remembering what Niko had told him when he came home alone from the honeymoon.

"I do not like fighting. I want to be with her. I am visiting her this weekend, but I fear she may decide to stay in Sachestia away from me."

"You have a duty—"

"To Vernonia."

"You also have a duty to your wife and your children." His father rose and came around to the front of his desk. "For years, I've told you to control your emotions and do what is best for Vernonia, but I'm not sure that is the advice I want you to give my grandchildren."

Niko wasn't sure he'd heard his father correctly. "What?"

"A united Vernonia has been the goal of kings for centuries, but united at what cost? Stefan's life? All the other sons and daughters and mothers and fathers who died during the conflict?" Regret filled his father's voice. "I wouldn't allow my own feelings to influence my decision-making. I kept telling myself what my father had told me. Emotion is a weakness. So I brushed aside my concerns over you and Stefan. Your mother's worries, too. Now each time I see the map of Vernonia on the wall over there, I wonder."

"Wonder what?" Niko asked, barely able to breathe.

"If I'd let the Separatists go, would Stefan still be alive today?"

Niko had never heard his father like this before. He stepped forward, unsure what to do. "Father—"

"That's why I had no choice but to see this through to the end and make sure you and Izzy remained married. I have to know if a united Vernonia is worth the sacrifices made. Especially your mother's broken and grief-filled heart."

"It will be, Father."

"I regret losing Stefan, but you have the traits of a good ruler, Niko. You will be a fine king."

He stood taller. "Thank you."

"But I am concerned," his father admitted. "You speak of modernizing the country, yet you hold old-fashioned notions. Especially your ideas of what a princess should be."

Isabel had said something similar. Uncomfortable, Niko shifted his weight between his feet.

"Izzy might not be a clone of every other princess out there, but she can still be who she is and the love of your life." His father pinned Niko with a hard stare. "The two are not mutually exclusive even if your marriage was an arranged match."

Niko considered his father's words. "The people—"

"She's more than made up for the lapse at the parade. Although I'm wondering if maybe she isn't the one who made the mistake. If perhaps we didn't give her enough credit. Did you know Queen Elizabeth II of the United Kingdom repaired vehicles during World War Two?"

The longtime and beloved monarch had been a mechanic like Izzy? Niko stiffened. "I did not."

"It is true." A thoughtful expression formed on his father's face. "The people in the north—Izzy's people—now love her exactly as she is."

"You have been spying on her."

His father raised a brow. "And you haven't?"

"I have sent two royal guards north to Sachestia on a brief...scouting trip."

"Thought so." He laughed. "You've always done whatever was asked of you, but it's time you were selfish. Forget everything else. Don't wait until this weekend to go to Sachestia. Do whatever it takes to save your marriage and keep Izzy in Vernonia, not through manipulation as I attempted, but through love and loyalty freely given."

"You want me to go after her now?"

"That's your decision, not mine." His father seemed to gaze off into the distance before focusing on Niko. "But if you have any feelings for your wife, allow nothing to keep you apart."

Niko had never allowed himself to be vulnerable with anyone before Izzy. He had opened up with her, but she wanted him to be vulnerable beyond the bedroom, to trust her in a way he had never trusted anyone before. Not even Stefan. And now they were having children... "I want to be with her, but I am still not sure how to make this work or how I feel."

"Figure it out. Fast." His father looked at a photograph of Stefan hanging on the wall. "Life can change in an instant, Niko. You don't want to have to live with that regret. Trust me."

Chapter Twenty-One

F*igure it out. Fast.*

What his father had said replayed in Niko's mind the rest of the day and evening. He wanted to figure it out. *Had* to figure it out.

But he needed to see Isabel, so he had asked Jovan to clear his calendar and arrange for the helicopter to fly him to Sachestia in the morning. Niko hoped he awoke with a plan in place because he had no idea what he would do or say after he arrived.

That night, he tossed and turned, drifting in and out of sleep. Images of Isabel, two babies, his father, his mother, and Stefan collided into a half-awake, half-dreamlike state. The bed lurched as if someone had shaken the entire wooden frame or rammed into it in the dark.

Had Isabel returned on her own?

Hope mushroomed in his chest like a nuclear blast.

Niko bolted upright, instantly awake. He glanced to the spot on his left. Still empty.

Disappointment squeezed his heart.

So far, the only thing Niko knew was what he had told his father. Niko missed her. He missed her smile, her laughter, her kisses, her warmth. He even missed the grease under her nails. He missed every fiber of her being, including the twin babies she now carried.

Wait. He glanced around the room. If Isabel hadn't shaken the bed... Something else must have caused it.

A knock sounded on his door.

"Enter."

Jovan, wearing a dark navy robe and slippers, rushed into the room, concern etched on his face. "There was an earthquake. They believe 6.8 on the Richter scale. The epicenter is in the north. In Sachestia."

Niko's gut knotted with fear. "Isabel?"

"We cannot contact the castle. All communications in the area are down."

He jumped out of bed and rushed to his closet. If he'd listened to his father, he would be with her. That was where Niko belonged. "I must go *now.*"

"The helicopter will be here in forty minutes."

He changed out of his pajama bottoms and into clothing. "Activate the emergency plan."

"Notifications went out as soon as confirmation of the earthquake was received."

His emergency response project was working properly, but he did not care. All his thoughts were focused on Isabel. On her well-being. Her safety. She had to be all right. And the babies. He buttoned his long-sleeved shirt. "I am going to see my father. I will meet you at the helipad."

He ran through the hallway toward his parents' suite.

Niko's stomach churned with fear and worry. Isabel could be lying, injured and alone, in the castle's rubble. If anything happened to her...

Life can change in an instant, Niko. You don't want to have to live with that regret. Trust me.

No regrets. Niko understood that part. He only hoped he was not too late.

He did not know if he could give Isabel the marriage she wanted, but he would give her all he could. He hoped, if she were safe and gave him the chance, what he offered would be enough.

The castle had survived the earthquake with minimal damage to the structure. Standing outside where cars were being loaded, Izzy brushed her hair out of her face. A stone wall had fallen and an old outbuilding collapsed, but nothing that couldn't be repaired. Several villages, however, had been near the epicenter. Reports of significant destruction and injuries streamed in. That meant they needed to move fast.

"Fill the truck with food, water, and blankets," Izzy instructed her staff, who carried supplies out of the castle. Some were dressed. Others wore their pajamas and robes. A chill hung in the night air. The sun wouldn't rise for two more hours. She zipped her jacket. "Hurry. We need to get up to the village ASAP."

"ASAP?" Emil asked.

"As soon as possible." She bent over to pick up a case of water. "I want to leave in five minutes."

"No, ma'am." Emil took the case from her hands and placed it into the truck. "I will see that the supplies arrive safely. You must stay here."

He sounded so much like Uncle Frank.

"I'm pregnant, not sick." Isabel had told a handful of the staff members what was going on in confidence. She patted her tummy. "The twins are safe and warm. I know what I can and can't do."

Emil eyed her warily. "The doctor—"

"Said I could continue my normal activities. Helping others in need is a normal activity."

Worry creased Emil's brow. "Prince Niko would not agree."

Hearing his name sent emotions swirling inside

Izzy. "Then it's good he's not here."

A part of her wished he was here, but at least he'd wanted to visit before her next appointment. That gave her hope things weren't over between them. At a time like this, differences and disagreements didn't seem as important as when she'd gone to bed.

"Supplies and help will be coming, but we're closest," she implored Emil. "We must go."

Emil nodded, respect gleaming in his eyes. "Your father and Franko would be proud of you, ma'am. I believe Prince Niko would be, too."

She doubted the latter, but appreciated Emil's compliment, anyway. "Thanks."

Duty was the most important thing to her husband. He seemed afraid to let himself go and lose control—or rather had been afraid until their fight after the parade. Izzy still couldn't forget the way he'd kissed her before he left. Full of emotion, brutal and punishing, the kiss seemed to betray the way he was also so strict with himself as prince. She wondered if he'd held his affection from her for that reason. Heaven knew she'd held herself back. She'd never told Niko she loved him. A mix of fear, pride, and stubbornness had kept her from declaring her feelings. Only knowing him for such a short time hadn't helped matters.

There's a lot at stake, Izzy. Don't let that stubborn streak of yours get in the way.

Rowdy's words echoed in her head. Maybe she had

been too stubborn. But there wasn't time for contemplation now. People needed help. She jumped into the truck. "Let's go."

Niko felt as if he had counted each heartbeat on the flight to Sachestia. That same heart went *splat* against the ground when he arrived at the castle.

Deserted.

No Isabel.

No staff.

No vehicles.

Broken vases, glasses, and sculptures littered the interior. Tipped-over bookcases and display cabinets lay haphazardly on the floor.

But no bodies. No blood.

Relief flowed through Niko. He leaned against the wall to catch his breath.

Jovan touched his shoulder. "The princess must have evacuated with the staff."

Not trusting his voice, Niko nodded.

Compassion filled Jovan's expression. "We'll find her."

Another nod. Niko's vision blurred. He blinked.

Fool.

That did not begin to describe how he had acted with Isabel. He had wasted so much time. Trying to do his duty when he should have been with his wife. She was what mattered most, but he had been too afraid to acknowledge that and now...

"Where could she—they—be?" His voice cracked.

"No one will allow anything to happen to her."

Niko wanted to believe him, but with so many villages in the area, ones that might be more damaged than the castle... "I pray that is true."

That she remained safe.

But what if she had been injured during the earthquake?

He gripped his stomach. The thought of her needing him…and he wasn't there…

"It is true," Jovan stated firmly. "We will find her."

Hours later, Niko was not any closer to locating his wife. He was not giving up, but he had to stop searching for Isabel to help others in immediate need.

Niko stepped through the rubble of one mountain village with a two-year-old child in his arms. The boy was cut and his pale skin bruised, but thankfully no broken bones.

The child cried. "Mama."

Niko did not know how to comfort the distraught boy who had been asleep under his bed when the earthquake hit. A neighbor had heard the boy's screams and pulled him from the rubble. Others were searching for the rest of his family. "The rescuers are looking for your mama."

The big, fat tears stopped rolling down the child's

face. He stared up at Niko. "Papa?"

"They are looking for him, too."

The boy rested his head against Niko's chest and placed his thumb in his mouth.

Niko swallowed around the lump of emotion in his throat.

A nurse appeared in sweat-stained surgical scrubs. "I'll take him, sir."

Reluctantly, he handed the injured boy to her. "His family is missing. Please..."

Don't lose him was what Niko wanted to say, given the number of people needing help and the chaos surrounding them.

She nodded in understanding. "We will take good care of him, sir."

With that, the nurse hurried into the hospital tent that had been erected next to the medical clinic.

Help continued to arrive. The sound of helicopters and heavy machinery filled the air.

His father was in another village helping, but Niko hoped the king saw a united Vernonia as Niko did.

Whether Separatist or Loyalist, people worked side by side, searching for survivors in the rubble and helping the injured. Differences in points of view or political opinions no longer mattered. They were all fellow Vernonians. Niko was so proud of the people. *His* people.

If only he knew where Isabel was... That she was safe...

A familiar-looking man caught his eye.

"Emil!"

The man turned and bowed. He held a can of oil. "Sir."

"Where is Isabel?"

Emil shifted uncomfortably. "She is safe, sir."

Safe was not good enough. Niko wanted his wife. He was a better man when he was with her. He needed her at his side. He would be a stronger, smarter prince. King, too.

The past no longer mattered. He did not care if Isabel preferred to work on cars or never wore a dress again. "Take me to her. Now."

The butler led Niko toward the medical tent. "Princess Izzy is attempting to fix the medical clinic's generator, sir. I tried to stop—"

Niko raised his hand. "I have learned nothing will stop my wife once she sets her mind upon something."

She wanted him to trust her, to let her figure out how to be a princess herself, but he had not known how to do that. He was ready now.

Emil grinned. "A true Vernonian."

"Yes, she is."

And the love of my life.

Chapter Twenty-Two

Years of dirt and grime coated the generator Izzy had found in the demolished storage area of the clinic. Villagers had carried the unit into an open area, eager for her to fix it with the makeshift toolkit they'd cobbled together. Izzy doubted if the generator had run in years or if it would have worked under the best of circumstances, but she had to try.

She studied the generator. A clamp hung off a pipe that didn't seem to be attached to anything. This wasn't like the car engines she was used to. She had no idea what she was doing.

Futility, frustration, and fatigue overwhelmed her determination. Her shoulders sagged.

This is too much for me. If Boyd or Rowdy were here…

No. Izzy pursed her lips. People were counting on her. She had to do this or patients needing medical treatment—surgeries—could die. She couldn't allow that to happen.

Kneeling, she ignored what she didn't understand and focused on what made sense. She checked a fuel line. "Come on. Show Izzy what's not right."

"Isabel."

Niko's voice washed over her like a ray of sunshine after a morning thunderstorm. Unexpected warmth flowed through her, and she knew the weeks apart hadn't erased her love for him. Despite their troubles.

"Hey." His being in the village didn't surprise her. He was the crown prince. This or one of the other affected villages was where he should be. But the vise grip on her heart wouldn't allow Izzy to peek in his direction. She stayed focused on the motor.

"You shouldn't be here," he said firmly.

Still telling her what to do. Well, she knew Niko wasn't Prince Charming.

Izzy blew out a puff of air.

"Don't worry, your heir and spare are safe." Her voice came out harsher than she intended, but she was struggling to keep herself together when a part of her wanted to run to Niko and have him hold her. She was stronger than that. "I would never do anything to risk the babies."

She had no doubt he cared about his children. His planning to visit once he found out about the pregnancy told her that. She only wished he cared as much about their mother, too.

The hurt stabbing her heart was beyond tears, but she needed to remain in control. Too many people were counting on her. Others needed Niko. This was not the time to discuss...anything.

The sounds of banging and metal crumpling surrounded them.

Izzy needed to stay focused. She slipped her hand inside a gap and tightened a loose coil.

Please work.

She tried the generator. It spurted but then started.

Thank goodness. But she didn't have time to celebrate. More needed to be done.

She wiped her hands on the oversized coveralls Boyd had sent her. On the left side, over her heart, *Princess Izzy* was embroidered in cursive writing. Her friend's way of saying thanks because Boyd loved his new truck.

"I know you would never put our children at risk," Niko said.

Kneeling, Izzy could see only his feet moving toward her. Her pulse quickened even if that was the last reaction to him she wanted to have right now.

Niko stopped. "But I cannot stand the thought of anything happening to *you*."

"Me?" Hope flared, but she tamped it down. She wouldn't be swayed by charm-laced words or his gorgeous face or his wide shoulders or blue-green... "You only married me because you had to."

"I could say the same thing about you."

At least he admitted it. As she stood, she tucked the thought away and then marched past him. "Come on."

He followed her, negotiating his way around the rubble.

She picked up two shovels and handed him one. "Know how to use one of these, Highness?"

"I do."

Izzy forced herself not to look at him. With so much work to be done, she needed to remain detached. She gestured with her own shovel. "Clear the rubble from the clinic's door."

"I want to talk to you."

She shut out any awareness of him. She couldn't afford the distraction. "Not now."

"What are you doing here?" He took her elbow with one hand.

"I'm doing what we're supposed to be doing." She shrugged away from him. "Helping our people."

With that, she walked away. Whatever he had to say could wait. Nothing had to be discussed now. Once lives were no longer at stake and the village not in a state of chaos, Niko could talk to her all he wanted.

Hours passed. Izzy worked, clearing, comforting,

and repairing whatever she was told to fix. She got another generator running.

Taking a break, she rubbed her lower back. The bending and kneeling had taken its toll, but the soreness was nothing compared to the injuries others faced.

As the sun sank below the horizon, red and orange splotches covered the sky like a watercolor. A beautiful sunset to contrast with the once quaint village square that looked as if a bomb had exploded. A handful of buildings survived intact. Most had walls missing. Some had collapsed to the ground in a heap of rubble. But help kept arriving from every direction. Rescuers found more survivors. This wasn't the end but a new beginning.

Niko handed her a bottle of water. "Drink."

She thought of the children lying in the hospital tent with tears streaming down their little faces. "Someone else might need it."

"You do. Drink." He shoved the bottle into her hands. "Additional supplies are on the way. The U.S., Aliestle, and other countries are sending help. Vernonia is not facing this natural disaster on its own. We have the world's help, and we will recover."

The strength behind his words impressed her.

"The people need to hear you say that." She sipped from the bottle. The refreshing water slid down her dry throat. "Okay, this tastes good. I needed it. Thanks."

"You've worked hard, Highness."

"So have you."

Izzy glanced Niko's way. His pants and jacket were ripped and dusty. Drops of blood were spattered on his sleeve. Stubble covered his dirty face. His tangled hair stuck up in different directions.

He'd never looked more like a prince than he did now.

Prince Charming couldn't hold a candle—or in this case, a shovel—to Prince Niko.

She swallowed a sigh and drank more water.

When she finished, Niko took her grease-covered, dirty hands in his.

Her heart hammered.

"Right now." His gaze locked on hers. "You look so much like the mechanic who walked out of that garage in Charlotte and stole my heart."

Her breath caught in her throat. "What?"

Affection shone in his eyes. "You are the most perfect princess I could hope to find."

Izzy half laughed. "Yeah, right. I look nothing like a princess."

"Exactly."

"Huh?"

"Isabel, Izzy, Princess, Highness, my wife. Your name does not matter." Niko pointed to her heart. "What matters is here. You have the heart of a princess."

Izzy was both excited and aggravated. He echoed what Jules had said.

You are a princess. You always have been. It's time you believed it. Not only in your mind, but also in your heart.

She wanted to believe that, but… "I—I don't know how to respond."

He shrugged. "'Thank you' might be a good start."

"Thanks, but why didn't you tell me this sooner?"

"I did not know. Or maybe I was not ready to admit the truth until now," he admitted. "I wanted to be honest with you and I was trying, but I was not honest with myself. I thought I knew what I was doing with my life. I had everything mapped out, and then this strange, kind, determined woman was thrust into my way and turned everything upside down."

"Strange?"

"Strange and beautiful." His smile sent tingles shooting through her. "You changed everything and left me uncertain how to act. Until now. I finally realize what a tremendous gift you are. And you are, Izzy. A gift and so much more. I never want you to doubt that—or yourself."

Izzy wanted to believe Niko. She'd seen glimpses of the man now standing in front of her since day one, but maybe it had taken a natural disaster for him to verbalize his feelings.

"When Uncle Frank died, I holed myself up and stuck with what was comfortable." She had been fine doing that because she hadn't known any better, but now… "You thrust me into this whole new world, and I've been trying to forge a path."

Niko squeezed her hand. "I am here. You do not have to forge your way alone. Together, we are stronger."

Izzy surveyed the devastation. But amid the rubble, signs of life, of love, appeared. "I know what Vernonia means to you. The land. These people. I may have been reluctant at first, but I'm here now because I understand this duty you are so attached to."

"A duty you are attached to as well."

She nodded.

"Our duty is not only to Vernonia. It is to each other and our children. That is the part I only recently realized. I am sorry I took so long, but I will never forget again." Niko's words made her heart sing. "I want you with me, Isabel. Always. I offer all that I have and all that I am. I hope that is enough."

The choice was hers. She could take what he was offering or leave it. They had much to work on and fix to bridge what had pushed them apart, but they had years—decades—to do that.

Together.

Izzy's heart overflowed with love. "I miss you, Niko. I don't want anything to stand in the way of us being together. We're better—stronger—standing side by side. I love you. I've loved you since our wedding day. I'm not sure what my role is supposed to be, but I'm ready to embrace it. With your help, maybe I won't fall flat on my face."

"You will not. I will not let you fall."

Izzy believed him.

As Niko gathered her into his arms, she went willingly, eager for his touch and his warmth. He lowered his mouth to hers, reclaiming her with a slow, hot kiss.

Her heart danced, dipping and twirling as if on a ballroom floor and not in a disaster zone.

"You are the only woman I want." His voice was so full of love she could barely breathe. "The only one I need. I love you. I want to marry you."

Izzy sank into his embrace. "We've already married. Twice."

"This time I want to exchange vows out of love, not duty or obligation. Nothing fancy. Just us." He placed his hand over her stomach with an almost reverent touch. "And these two."

"Yes! I'd like that very much." Laughter spilled from her lips. "Maybe the third time, we'll get it right."

"If not, we will try again until we do." The depth of the affection written on his face sent her pulse skyrocketing. "I am never letting you go, Highness."

"You can't even if you want to, Highness." She grinned. "In case you forgot, your bridal box, the key, and you are mine."

Epilogue

Izzy cradled His Royal Highness Prince Aleksander Stefan, the future heir to the Vernonian throne, in her arms. Contentment and peace flowed through her. The baby slept with a serene expression on his beautiful face, a face that reminded Izzy of her beloved husband. She kissed her son's tiny forehead, inhaling the baby scent she never imagined could smell so sweet.

Niko carefully adjusted a blue cap on His Royal Highness Prince Franko Stefan's head. The adoration on her husband's face sent a burst of joy through her.

The sight of her loving husband and two healthy sons made her heart overflow with happiness. Izzy exhaled on a sigh. Life couldn't get much better.

She'd spent the months of her pregnancy figuring out her role as a princess and a wife. She much preferred the latter role, but the former was growing on her as she assisted the areas devastated by the earthquake and found a way to maintain "Izzy" while also being "Princess Isabel."

Through it all, Niko had been at her side since the earthquake. Village walls hadn't been the only ones knocked down by the tremors. Niko had opened his heart to her, and there was no going back.

Was everything perfect?

No, both of them were still learning about being married. Compromises and mistakes were made. Apologies and forgiveness given. But she finally understood what happily ever after meant. She was living the fairy tale and felt blessed by all she'd been given from Vernonia, her people, and Niko.

Especially him.

Niko stared lovingly at the child in his arms. "Franko is asleep."

"So is Alek."

Their gazes met in unspoken understanding. Between the nursing and diapering, getting both babies to sleep at the same time was a coup. But they were in this thing called parenting together, and Izzy couldn't imagine a better partner. Niko had embraced the role of husband and father, not out of duty, but with his whole heart.

Niko's expression clouded with concern. "The noise—"

"The pediatrician assured me we're high enough from the crowd the decibel level won't be a problem."

"I was more worried about them waking up."

"They eventually will need to get used to noise and the attention."

"The boys are lucky to have such a knowledgeable princess as their mother." Niko's grin made her heart leap. "And I'm the most fortunate man in the world to call you my wife."

She winked. "Just so you know, the feeling's mutual, Highness."

Desire gleamed in his eyes. "If only we didn't have to—"

"But we do. Duty calls." She moved toward the arched balcony doors of the Parliament building. "It's time to introduce Vernonia to their new princes."

Niko smiled mischievously. "You know what I'd rather do."

He eyed her as if he'd been lost in the desert and she were a glass of water, leaving no doubt in Izzy's mind what he wanted to do. But she was still healing from delivering twins. "The doctor said it wouldn't be much longer."

Niko's gaze went to each of their sons before resting on her. "Worth the wait."

"Good answer."

He winked. "I'm learning."

"Yes, you are. You can swaddle and diaper like a pro now."

"As can my father."

Dee and Bea both wanted to take active roles in the twins' daily lives. The castle had never been so busy. Izzy couldn't imagine when the boys crawled or walked.

"What do you think of having princesses or more princes in the future?" Niko asked.

She pursed her lips. "I suppose you can never have too many spares. Besides, we need enough for a racing team."

"A team, not a pit crew?"

"A princess can dream."

"Bringing F-one racing to Vernonia isn't enough?"

Niko had told her to present the concept of a race in the capitol city to his father. She had, and the king agreed. The race wouldn't happen until next season, but hotel reservations were already up. The unexpected boost in the economy was turning into a huge positive.

Niko kissed her. Only a quick brush of the lips, but it would do.

For now.

His blue-green eyes stared deeply into hers. No way would she ever doubt his love. Not for a second.

Izzy smiled up at him. "You can never have too much family."

About the Author

USA Today bestselling author Melissa McClone has written over forty-five sweet contemporary romance novels and been nominated for Romance Writers of America's RITA® Award. She lives in the Pacific Northwest with her husband, three children, two spoiled Norwegian Elkhounds, and cats who think they rule the house. They do! If you'd like to learn more about Melissa, please visit www.melissamcclone.com or email her at melissa@melissamcclone.com. You can find Melissa on Facebook at melissamcclonebooks and her McClone Troopers Reader Facebook Group or connect with her on Twitter @melissamcclone and Instagram @melmcclone

Other Books by Melissa McClone

SERIES
All series stories are standalone,
but past characters may show up.

Her Royal Duty Series
Royal romances with
charming princes and dreamy castles...
The Accidental Princess
The Reluctant Princess
The Not-So-Perfect Princess
The Proper Princess

Mountain Rescue Series
Finding love in Hood Hamlet
with a little help from Christmas magic…
His Christmas Wish
Her Christmas Secret
Her Christmas Kiss
His Second Chance
His Christmas Family

The Bar V5 Ranch Series
Fall in love at a dude ranch in Montana…
Home for Christmas
Mistletoe Magic
Kiss Me, Cowboy
Mistletoe Wedding
A Christmas Homecoming

Quinn Valley Ranch
Relatives in a large family find love in Quinn Valley, Idaho…
Carter's Cowgirl

One Night to Forever Series
Can one night change your life…
and your relationship status?
Fiancé for the Night
The Wedding Lullaby

Beach Brides & Indigo Bay Sweet Romance Series
A mini-series within two multi-author series…
Jenny
Sweet Holiday Wishes
Sweet Beginnings

Ever After Series
Happily ever after reality TV style…
The Honeymoon Prize
The Cinderella Princess
Christmas in the Castle

Love at the Chocolate Shop Series
Three siblings find love thanks to
Copper Mountain Chocolate…
A Thankful Heart
The Valentine Quest
The Chocolate Touch

STANDALONE
Sigh-worthy sweet contemporary romances...
Picture Perfect Love
The Christmas Window